M000076810

GRIND

POWERTOOLS: THE ORIGINAL CREW RETURNS, BOOK 3

JAYNE RYLON

HAPPY ENDINGS PUBLISHING

V2

eBook ISBN: 978-1-947093-19-5

Print ISBN: 978-1-947093-20-1

Cover Design by Jayne Rylon

Editing by Mackenzie Walton

Proofreading by Fedora Chen

Formatting by Jayne Rylon

ABOUT THE BOOK

The original Powertools crew is back in a brand new series!

The crew has overcome enormous odds to live and love together. Can it survive being divided?

Dave knows where he's needed most is back home, helping his wife rebuild her business—and her dreams—which burned to the ground while they were partying with friends. But is it right to expect their friends Devon, Neil, and James to be there too if it means giving up opportunities to join Mike and Joe on the project of a lifetime in Middletown? And how will they manage on their own if not?

Resentment could be the final nail in the crew's coffin if they can't find a way to move forward together. Because in addition to their careers, the Powertools' intimate bond is in jeopardy. It's up to them to find a way to strengthen it even if it means grinding away at the past in order to prepare for a bright future.

This is a standalone book set in the Powertools universe. All your favorite Hot Rods and Hot Rides characters will be making appearances as well. So come make new book boyfriends or hang out with old ones!

ADDITIONAL INFORMATION

Sign up for the Naughty News for contests, release updates, news, appearance information, sneak peek excerpts, reading-themed apparel deals, and more. www.jaynerylon.com/newsletter

Shop for autographed books, reading-themed apparel, goodies, and more www.jaynerylon.com/shop

A complete list of Jayne's books can be found at www.jaynerylon.com/books

1

Smoke rose from the charred wreckage of Kayla's dreams. It curled upward like the tentacles of some sinister monster from hell, threatening to drag her into its dark and fiery underworld. She was suffocating.

Orange clouds and eerie limited visibility lingered in the aftermath of the deadly forest fire that had swept the surrounding mountains. It only added to her inability to draw a deep breath. Not that there was much left to see beyond the ominous haze.

It was gone. Every last bit of her naturist resort—the cabins, the home she'd shared with her husband for fourteen years, the lodge. Even the trees and animals that had infused them with serenity and tranquility to observe.

Their future.

All of it had gone up in the blaze that had decimated thousands of acres in a matter of hours.

Smoke and flames. So. Many. Flames.

"Thank God the resort was closed and we were in Middletown at Ollie, Van, and Kyra's wedding. This would have been so much worse if there was anyone here. Guests. Us." Her husband Dave's voice was even deeper and raspier than usual, whether from the thick char poisoning the air or his emotions, she couldn't tell.

Kayla blamed her watering eyes on the soot and not the blackness settling in her heart as it had on everything around them. How could they possibly come back from this?

Along with her agony, anger began to smolder in her core. They'd worked so hard all these years. And for what? For it to be stolen from them overnight, destroyed before they'd even known it was in jeopardy.

She blinked, then blinked again. But nothing changed.

This was a nightmare she couldn't wake up from.

Behind them, Neil, James and Devon stepped closer, as if their presence could somehow shield them from the horror of what they were seeing and the things they were not. How could her entire life's work disappear with hardly a trace? The dense wall of smoke made it impossible to spot the lake in the distance, the panoramic views obliterated as surely as everything else on the mountainside.

It was probably for the best. If she could scan the horizon and it was only more of this unrelenting scorched earth that greeted her, Kayla would likely be driven to her knees. How could this have happened? It seemed like a movie or the apocalypse.

It certainly didn't seem real.

She wandered over the gravel that had been their driveway, which now only led to a vague outline of a square on the ground. The ashes of her home were interrupted by a single stone pillar, crumbled a bit on top, which had been the mammoth hearth at the heart of their home. Melted blobs of steel marked the place where the kitchen had stood.

Memories smashed into her one after the other. The Powertools crew get-togethers. Special meals they'd cooked and shared. And the times they'd made love on the plush rugs right there, in front of that fireplace.

Kayla shuddered. She'd never be able to see flames, controlled or not, in the same cozy way again.

Some things had been ruined forever.

The trick was going to be figuring out what damage was irreparable and what she could fix. Or maybe she was kidding herself. This was too much. Too impossible to come back from.

She sank onto the bench that had been part of their fireplace and dropped her face into her hands. She had to block out the devastation, at least for a second, or she was going to suffocate. It became harder to breathe when her body began to hitch and sobs burst from her chest.

"I'm here." Dave plunked down beside her and gathered her to his side. He surrounded her in his massive arms, though for once in their lives, he couldn't protect her. Not from this.

She held as much of him as she could, clinging to his warmth and strength like a baby koala. His love was like this hearth, her rock, unwavering and indestructible, even in the face of so much adversity.

Of course they argued, like every couple, but never for long, and they always made up afterward. Hugging him tight enough that she could detect his familiar scent through the wall of smoke finally made her be able to draw in a shaky breath and then another, her tears eventually drying up enough that she could focus on the world around her again.

JAYNE RYLON

Devon, Neil, and James stood guard, each of them looking worried as hell as they took in Kayla and the utter wreckage strewn across the mountaintop.

Kayla concentrated on filling her lungs again without choking, then separated herself from Dave, pushing to her feet. She wiped her shaking palms on her jeans and said, "I don't know how, but I'll find a way to bring it back. To put it right. To make it again like it was before."

"Kayla, we're in this together," Dave reminded her, standing too and resting his hands on her shoulders, squeezing lightly.

"Whatever you need, we're here for you," Devon echoed. Neil and James nodded their agreement.

While their immediate and steadfast support should have reassured her, instead it only caused some of her uneasiness to creep back in like the insidious smoke that wafted all around, filling every breath with a reminder of what had happened, and the hurdles she was going to face. "That's what I'm afraid of. I don't want to drag you all with me on some impossible mission when you have opportunities to do more, make something new for yourselves instead."

For nearly two decades, the Powertools construction crew—made up of Dave, Devon, James, Neil, and two of their best friends, Joe and Mike—had worked together day in and day out, building their own business from the ground up. Recently, Joe had taken a chance a few states away to help his cousin expand Hot Rods, the guy's classic car restoration garage, and the living quarters for its mechanics. They also happened to be in a poly relationship not so different from the one Kayla and Dave shared with the crew.

One thing had led to another, and soon their foreman,

4

Mike, had also been approached with a new business opportunity, overseeing the construction of a tattoo shop and tourism destination that could become the Midwestern version of Gatlinburg if he played his cards right. Each member of the crew could step up and run their own crew if they wanted, expanding their empire and transitioning into work that paid better without taxing their bodies as much as they got older. There was enough work, and they were skilled as hell.

Would it be selfish of her to take four of their team members and keep them for herself?

Dave was first to cut her off and keep her from going farther down that road paved with guilt and self-doubt. "Hey, you remember after my accident, I felt the same way? Like I was a burden or some shit? And what did you tell me over and over?"

He used his grip on her shoulders and turned her so that she had to look at him instead of the embers, which used to be her vision come to life. A place where they and others had been so damn happy. But it hadn't always been that way.

Kayla thought back to the dark times Dave was talking about, which seemed much less scary now that they'd passed and she and Dave had put their troubles years behind them. "That if you gave up I'd never forgive you."

"Right. And what else?"

"That you could get back what you'd lost, even if it didn't look quite the same. That we would work on it together and get a little stronger every day. That life would be worth living again." Kayla got a little annoyed at herself even as she said it, because she remembered how scared she'd been then for him and worried she might be making him equally as afraid now.

She didn't do self-pity. At least not usually.

"Exactly." Dave drew her into his arms and surrounded her in a warm embrace. "And that's what we're going to do. You and me and..."

He trailed off then, peeking over her head at Devon, James, and Neil. Just because they'd always been best friends didn't mean that she expected them to sacrifice their careers and their futures for her dream. Not even Dave could, or should, make them promise more than they were willing to give on their own.

This, Bare Natural, had been the only thing holding Dave, Kayla, and the rest of the crew in their hometown. With the developments cropping up in Middletown, maybe they would see this as an omen, the push they needed to make a permanent change.

Kayla wouldn't blame them one bit if they decided this was where their paths diverged.

Devon stepped forward then ducked under Dave's arm, so he was hugging them both. Devon might be petite, but she was fierce and determined as hell. Whatever she committed to, her guys would go along with it. Hell, more like they'd likely feel the same. The three of them were so close, it was hard to separate them sometimes. "'Kay, come on. You know we're here for you. For as long as you need, we'll stay. We'll work. We'll make this right again."

"No, not just that. But better than before." James swooped in closer and put his hand on Kayla's back, rubbing lightly.

Neil squeezed Dave's shoulder. "You're not alone. None of us is ever alone when we're part of the crew. Even if we're spread out right now, that hasn't changed."

Kayla melted in Dave's arms, going lax in his hold as

their reassurances sank in. Then and only then, did she start to cry again. This time out of relief.

"You're breaking my heart," Dave murmured to her.

But when she sniffled and raised her head, there was a fire at least as bright as the one that had razed the land now burning in her core. "You're right. All of you. I'm not a quitter. I'm not giving up on this place or this dream. This is my whole life. I can do this...if you'll help me."

"We will. Of course we will." Dave leaned his forehead on hers and smiled softly. "*This* is the woman I love. My partner. And as long as we have each other, nothing is impossible. You brought me back from the brink of death, held my hand as I learned to walk again. And now, maybe, I can repay you a little."

"I love you," she whispered because anything else seemed too frivolous for the emotions charging through her.

"I love you too." He sealed the promise with a kiss.

Devon, James, and Neil surrounded them in a group hug, and Kayla began to believe there was a way forward for them all. Together.

2

———

They'd stayed for a while longer, documenting the damage with pictures and videos from all angles to share with the insurance company and their friends in Middletown. Every time Kayla clicked the shutter button she tried to imagine what had been there before and how she would not only put it back but enhance it.

It took a lot of emotional energy, though, and before too long she was exhausted and ready to go...well, where she wasn't sure, since *home* was out of the question.

She ambled over to the van they'd ridden in together from Middletown, where they'd gotten the terrible news before the ass crack of dawn. Devon must be even more wiped than she was. They hadn't gotten a lot of sleep the night before and she'd driven the whole way, most of it in the dark.

Devon turned her head and stifled a yawn with the back of her hand. Kayla felt it straight to her soul. "We can get out of here. There's nothing else I can do right now and I'm sure you'd like to take a nap."

"You guys staying with us or what?" Devon asked Kayla and Dave.

"Honestly, I hadn't even thought that far ahead." Kayla looked into the backseat of the van at the tiny black rolling suitcase she'd packed for their weekend getaway. "That's all we own. Wow. I guess..."

Still numb, she looked over at Dave, and he nodded. "Thanks. Yeah. It'll be nice to be somewhere familiar while we get this figured out. And if you get tired of us long-term, feel free to kick us out at any point."

"I doubt that's going to happen." Neil snorted. "I mean, let's set a goal to make Mike, Kate, Joe, and Morgan as jealous of us as I am of them. Maybe we can start some kind of sex tournament."

The crew was divided, but at least no one was alone.

"I see where you're going. Two teams. Of course, we have an advantage with five people to their four..." James was already sketching out the rules for their sexual Olympics as he hopped into the passenger seat. Whether he was indulging Neil's somewhat immature and always funny side in the hopes of distracting them from the shit sandwich they'd been served or he really thought it was a good idea, he ran with the idea while Devon and Neil joined him in the van.

Dave's big hands encircled Kayla's waist. He boosted her into the vehicle, where she sat between him and Neil. The heat from their bodies, which bracketed her, soothed her as they rolled carefully out of their long driveway and then down the mountain.

Eventually dead earth gave way to golden grasses and then the wildflowers of late summer lower in the valley near town, where Devon, Neil, and James lived. Kayla leaned on Dave, her head resting on his shoulder as she let her friends' brainstorming and laughter swirl around her. She couldn't have repeated a single thing they said, but it felt nice for at least one thing to be normal.

And when they pulled into their driveway, Kayla considered lying down on the bench seat of the van rather than wasting effort on walking into the house. Exhaustion made her bones feel four times as heavy as usual.

"Come on." Dave took her hand and eased her to the doorway before lifting her into his arms. He didn't do that often given that she was the tallest and heaviest of the Powertools women—hell, she probably weighed more than James—and his balance wasn't always terrific.

"Thanks, but I can walk." She squirmed until he put her down, stealing a quick kiss almost as a reflex. He looped his arm around her waist and supported her until they'd made it inside and she'd kicked off her dirty sneakers.

She oozed onto Devon's couch and wondered if she could camp out there until the insurance company opened the next morning. She was going to need every bit of energy she could muster to sort through this mess.

"I'm going to cook us something," James said as he headed for the kitchen. "Anyone have a preference?"

"Don't worry about me." Kayla waved him off. It would be a miracle if she could swallow around the lump in her throat.

"Oh, I'm plenty concerned." James blew her a kiss. "I'm going to make grilled cheese and tomato soup."

"I'm not sick." She couldn't help but smile a bit at his kindness. They all knew it was her favorite when she was under the weather.

"Nope, you're sad and that's even harder to watch. So

you're going to eat my damn sandwich and act like you like it."

Kayla laughed. "Okay, fine."

It didn't take him long to whip up a tray for them all to share, but the whole time he was working on it, Neil, Devon, and Dave did their best *this-is-fine-everything's-fine* imitation to keep her mind off of the disaster. For the most part, it worked. And it only made her more grateful that she had such close friends, and lovers, to lean on when she needed them most.

When they'd finished eating—her stomach feeling decidedly less churny after being sated with warm, yummy cheese, bread, and soup—Neil collected their plates. He put a palm on her shoulder as he reached over her to collect her dishes.

"Damn, you've got knots in those arms bigger than Dave's muscles. Good thing I know an excellent masseuse and she's taught me a thing or two." He grinned down at her. "Let me finish cleaning up and I'll work on them if you want."

Kayla closed her eyes and nodded. "Thank you. I don't know what I would do without you guys. This is probably the worst day of my life, but I'll get through it because of you."

"I remember the first time we were all together," Dave told her. "During that massive blizzard. Things seemed grim then too. Not like this, but scary nonetheless."

"You did a hell of a job distracting me that weekend." Kayla laughed softly as she looked from her husband to two of his closest friends. Neil and James had conspired to bring them together, although she hadn't know it at the time. And yes, all these years later, she was so glad they had. They'd seen what Dave and Kayla had been ignoring for too long and gave them the nudge it had taken to come together. Permanently.

"My guys are willing to take your mind off things any time you need," Devon promised her, then elbowed Neil in the ribs, only sort of joking. "Aren't you, stud muffin?"

Kayla snorted at that. These were her people. They knew exactly what she needed and how to give it to her. Even when she couldn't have told them what that entailed. They understood, because they knew her and loved her.

Entrusting herself fully to their care, she lifted her arms to Dave and let him drag her into his lap and his embrace. "Feel free to do your best. But don't blame me if it doesn't work. I'm so fucked up."

"You're not." Devon got out of her chair and circled around the table to stand next to Dave. She hugged him and Kayla too. "What you're feeling is normal. It's grief. Let us do what we can to help you through it."

Kayla nodded then angled her head toward Devon. The other woman always understood her. She sighed when Devon leaned in and kissed her, just for a moment, a brief ghosting of her lips over Kayla's, as if she was afraid of breaking her. "You're going to be okay. We're going to ride this out."

Neil stroked Devon's hair, then put his hand on her shoulder. "Why don't we take this upstairs?"

Devon nodded and held her arms out to him. He scooped her up and tucked her against his chest before turning toward James and saying, "Let's go."

James was right on Neil's heels, or maybe his ass, as they headed for the stairs that led to their bedroom. Dave lifted Kayla and cradled her as he followed silently. When she squirmed this time, he refused to put her down, not even for a moment.

"Are *you* okay?" Kayla murmured to him as they ascended. "It was your home too. Your life."

"I think I'm still in shock." He sighed. "I'm just glad I have you."

Kayla stroked his neck and relished the stubble that prickled her palm. If it was slightly silvered now compared to the dark hair he'd had when they first met, she thought it only made him more handsome. His accident had aged him, changed him in ways she maybe hadn't fully understood until right now.

The sense of loss she felt was so overwhelming, it was like trying to constantly swim for the surface of their dark, cool lake except with lead weights on her ankles. And yet, he'd done this before. He'd endured. He'd survived. Of course he was better equipped than her to deal with trauma, but that didn't mean he didn't need support too.

"We're going to make it better," she promised him. "We're together. We're safe. You're right. That's all that really matters."

He nodded, then dropped his head to kiss her as he neared the edge of Devon, James, and Neil's enormous custom-made bed, plenty big enough for the throuple plus any guests they might have over.

"See, I told you this bed was a smart choice. Function over form, baby." Neil grinned as he teased James, who had taken the monstrosity as a personal insult to his tasteful decorating of their home.

"Fine. Every once in a while you're right."

"Things don't always have to be pretty to be perfect." It wasn't often that Neil was serious for long enough to be the wise-sounding one of the bunch, but right then Kayla thought he had nailed it.

Her life was a hot mess. But that didn't mean it wasn't still amazing, and that she couldn't transform it into something even more amazing than what it had been if she kept her husband and her friends close. They could do this. They always had before and she didn't see that changing any time soon.

She groaned.

"You okay?" Dave asked.

"Missing the rest of the crew." Kayla tried not to think of how far away Mike, Kate, Joe, and Morgan were when she needed them too. It would only make her upset again and that was bullshit. She refused to shed one more tear that day. And she never intended to make them feel guilty about smashing their own goals.

James sighed. "You'll have to settle for us."

"That's not what I meant." Kayla bit her lip as Dave set her on the bed then followed her down.

"I know." James climbed onto the mattress on her other side and kissed her, a little more thoroughly than his wife had in their living room a few minutes ago. "I miss them too. That's what I should have said."

"This is a lot. For everyone. I hate that we're apart, especially right now when we need each other most." Neil set Devon down, then laced his fingers with hers and led her to the bed. Together they climbed on from the foot of the massive square and knelt near Dave, Kayla, and James's feet.

In that moment, Kayla realized this wasn't only for her. Bonding, sharing like they were about to do, was for them too. The crew felt most grounded when they were one unit, when they enjoyed each other and the links between them. For a little while at least, she found her purpose.

This was something she could do to make things better, not only for herself.

Kayla rolled to her back and began to shove her shirt up and over her head. She would give all of herself gladly if it meant any of them suffered less. And twice as eagerly because she knew that whatever she put out there would be returned to her four times over.

It wasn't often she craved being the center of attention, preferring to watch one of the others be spoiled, but right then she needed the intensity of their combined advances to pull her away from the hole in her heart.

And they seemed more than willing to fill the void inside her.

Dave's eyes turned steely and she squirmed as he went into what she thought of as his sexy beast mode. He was usually pretty laidback, but every once in a while—like now—he took charge, and never had he disappointed her when he did.

Kayla surrendered to him, their friends, and everything they were about to do to her. She allowed her mind to disengage and resorted to reacting purely on emotion. Something she would never have thought herself capable of trusting enough to do when she'd been younger.

Growing up, she hadn't had the kind of upbringing that taught her about unconditional closeness. Her parents had always been busy with important careers, and her brothers and sisters had followed suit. Lawyers, doctors, you know...definitely not a freaky tattooed-and-pierced owner of a naturist resort.

But now, with these people who'd chosen her, she

finally believed they cared for her enough to let go and believe they would catch her.

Kayla wasn't sure when they'd ditched their clothes, but she moaned softly at the feel of Neil's smooth skin pressing to hers all along her back. His hand caressed her hip before slipping around to the side of her ass. He nuzzled the crook of her neck as he ground against her, letting her feel how ready he was to find his way inside.

"Is that what you want?" Dave asked. "You want us both to fuck you at the same time? To be full of us, working together to make you come?"

It had been a while since she'd been at the center. Which only made it that more appealing. "Yeah. That. Do that."

She glanced over her shoulder at Neil, who smiled wide before pressing his lips to hers. He wasn't the most gentle or the most suave, but she never doubted how he felt about her—eager and enthusiastic.

James approached with a bottle in his hand and said, "Here, let me help."

He was a pro, loving anal as much as any of the rest of the crew. He would make sure it was only pleasurable when his husband slipped into her. Thankfully Neil wasn't as much to handle as her husband because she was sure Dave would be stretching her pussy as soon as she settled onto Neil.

Goose bumps broke out on her arms and her nipples tightened in anticipation. Maybe she wasn't as damaged as she'd thought. Or maybe they were just that good at putting her back together.

Devon chuckled. "They are pretty amazing, my guys, aren't they?"

She caressed Kayla's neck, then brushed her hair away

from her eyes so that they could share a secret smile along with the men they had both loved for so long now. Hell, and each other.

Kayla turned her face so she could kiss Devon's palm. "Thanks for lending them to me."

"You know I love watching them like this, doing their thing." Devon sighed and ran her hand over her flat stomach, honed by years of labor on the crew.

Kayla was distracted from Devon's feminine six-pack when Neil groaned. The slick sounds of flesh on flesh made her look over in time to see James slathering Neil's hard-on with lube. And then it was her turn. James brushed his thumb over her ass, acclimatizing her to his touch before he got more intimate, running his glossy fingers through her crack, then rubbing the puckered muscles at the center.

He guided the tip of his finger inside her, making sure to ease the way for his husband, who would no doubt follow close behind. She couldn't wait.

3

——————

Dave rubbed against Kayla. Their chests aligned as he watched his friends preparing her to be joined with them. His breathing picked up, and so did the weight of his cock against her stomach.

Kayla reached for him, surrounding him as best she could with her hand and stroking him the rest of the way to full erection. He cursed softly, then dipped his chin to kiss her. And as he stole her concentration with the gentle lap of his tongue over her parted lips and a sweet yet steamy kiss only he knew how to give her, the blunt head of Neil's cock replaced James's fingers.

He nudged her, grasping her hip to keep her in place as he began to work inside her ass.

Kayla might have frozen as the pressure grew, simultaneously making her want to push back against Neil and scurry away, if Dave hadn't been there to thaw her, kissing her with more passion than she had a right to ask for. She opened her eyes to look directly into his as their friend embedded himself within her fully and left her wanting so much more from her husband.

As if he understood, Neil wrapped his arm around her waist, hugging her tight to his chest before he rolled, taking her with him as he settled onto his back. He used his legs between hers to spread her wide open in invitation. One Dave didn't hesitate to accept.

James's hand was trapped between Neil and Kayla. He drew a circle around Neil's cock where it was fitted into her ass, making both of them gasp and her eyes threaten to roll back in her head. Then he ran his palms down her front from her shoulders, over her breasts, to her stomach, and across her mound. Kayla squirmed, impaling herself deeper on Neil's cock in the process.

Fuck, that felt so good. But she needed something more intense for euphoria to usurp her anxiety and heartache and give her relief from the tragedy that had befallen them.

Dave growled to James, "Keep doing that. Make her feel good. This is going to be a lot and we haven't done this in a while."

James nodded. "I have you covered."

He rotated around, his leg passing in front of Kayla's face as he knelt above her, now with his mouth hovering over her pussy and his cock hanging between her breasts. Devon smacked his ass, and the sharp crack did nothing to decrease the stiffness of his erection. A bead of precome formed at the head of his cock and dripped onto Kayla's breast.

Devon swiped it away before massaging it into James's skin. "That's right, baby. Go down on Kayla. Lick her clit while Dave fucks her and Neil fills that sexy ass. Make her come so hard that they can't help but lose it inside her. If you're a good boy, she might let you ride her chest. I know

how much you love to feel her tits on your dick, don't
you?"

Kayla's brows rose as she looked up at Devon, who
shrugged. Lately she'd been getting more and more
assertive, setting record levels on the sass-o-meter. If Kayla
hadn't been in the middle of a very delicate—in all the
right ways—situation, she might have wondered if
Devon's transformation had something to do with what
Joe and Mike were up to in Middletown and how much
more control she had taken of the remaining Powertools
crew in their absence. Regardless of why it had occurred,
her husbands certainly seemed to appreciate the change.

James made an unintelligible sound that somehow
conveyed everything they needed to know. He loved being
bossed around. Being ordered to bring them pleasure
amplified his own satisfaction.

Kayla reached down and squished her breasts
together, welcoming him into the valley she created. He
shuddered and settled in, his breath washing over her clit
as he squeezed between her tits. He wasn't the most well
endowed of the crew, but it was the skill in using the tool,
not the size of it that mattered.

And his mouth...

That was talented as fuck.

James swirled his tongue around her clit, easing her
into his touch. He coordinated with Dave, and when her
husband gave him the signal, James covered her aching
flesh with his mouth and sucked gently. Dave rode the
furrow of her pussy and then used three fingers to push
his cock down so the tip began to wedge inside her
opening instead of gliding past it.

Kayla cried out when the fullness of Neil in her ass and

the mass of her husband joining him stretched her to her limits. Immediately, everyone stopped. Neil hugged her, stroking her arms while Dave cupped her knees, rubbing the insides of them with his thumbs. James massaged her flanks and nuzzled her mound. Even Devon stroked the hair off her forehead and cheeks, murmuring encouragement.

In that moment, everything clicked into place. Kayla drew the first deep breath she had since the phone had rung in the middle of the night and the police chief had informed her that her life would never be the same again. She was surrounded, and filled, by people who loved her, who wouldn't let anything hurt her, who would help her get through even the worst of times.

She relaxed, and Dave slipped deeper inside.

"That's right. Let me in," he coached her as he began to move again. Slowly, gently, while peering intently down at her face. He shifted his gaze to Devon, who nodded to both him and Neil.

"She's okay. You can go," Devon told her husband.

"And what about you?" Neil asked her.

"I'm enjoying the show." She grinned. "Don't worry, I can take care of myself."

"That's not the Powertools way." Dave grimaced even as he burrowed another inch or two into Kayla.

James looked over his shoulder and said, "There's room... Why don't you let Neil taste you and see how wet you are from watching us?"

Neil's cock twitched in Kayla's ass, inspiring her moan. "He likes that idea. Do it, Dev."

Between Neil, James, and Dave, they adjusted themselves and Kayla so that Neil was at a slight angle to Kayla's body. His torso and arm still made an extra comfy pillow, cradling her for Dave and James to make love to, but left room for Devon to kneel over his head. Her thigh lined up next to Kayla's cheek, creating the perfect place for her to rest her head.

Neil groaned and must have given Devon a similar treatment to the one James treated her to, gauging by the wet sounds of his tongue and lips on the other woman's flesh. A tremor of desire ran through Kayla, curling her toes.

Dave grinned down at her. He withdrew a bit then slid home, beginning to properly fuck her instead of simply warming her up and accustoming her to his presence.

James's ass clenched and his cock slipped more easily between her breasts as his precome lubricated the sides of them. His abs raked over the piercings in her nipples, shooting zings of pleasure through her.

Kayla couldn't focus on anything except the way her lovers were making her feel and none of the things they did were bad or painful. They were all so very good. It was such a relief.

She sighed and writhed, trying to get closer to each of them.

Devon reached out and rubbed James's ass, which glowed red where she'd spanked him earlier. He rocked back into her touch and sucked Kayla's clit a little harder. His next thrust across her chest made her hardware tug on her nipples and set off another sensual chain reaction where she hugged Neil and Dave in response.

"Fuck yes," Dave growled, and Neil groaned against Devon's pussy. "Pet him again, Devon."

"I can do better than that." She laughed, sounding like a mischievous pixie more than a badass construction worker.

She reached to the side, her hand blindly finding the

drawer of the nightstand and opening it. The racket that followed made Kayla sure Devon was fishing around for something in particular. And she must have found it, because she said, "Ah ha!"

When she brandished a curved vibrator where Kayla could see it, she recognized it as one of James's favorite prostate stimulating toys. Things were about to get interesting.

Kayla spread her knees and hooked her heels in the small of Dave's back, encouraging him to plunge deeper, harder, and faster within her. Neil needed no encouragement. He gripped her hips and thrust upward, devouring his wife even as she prepared to insert her tool into their husband's ass, which was on prominent display.

Kayla would be lying if she said, even after all this time, that it didn't turn her on to witness the guys surrender to each other or—in this case—to one of the women. She loved how it fired them up to fuck each other and how ass play took their sessions to the next level.

If her hands hadn't been pinned to her sides by the delicious weight of James lying over her like a security blanket, she would have offered to assist Devon with inserting the toy and using it to give James as much pleasure as he was giving her.

But the truth was, Devon didn't need any help. She rose up enough to allow Neil to suck the thin, curved wand with a vibrating bulge at the tip, coating it with his saliva, before tapping it against James's clenching hole. James lifted his head and cried out, his face mashing against Dave's abs. Dave kept fucking into Kayla while kneeling between her thighs.

Dave cupped James's cheek and rasped, "That's right,

Devon's going to give it to you. Make my wife come first, before you make a mess of her. You hear me?"

James nodded, then licked Dave's abs, the best he could do at communicating some kind of coherent response, before returning his attention to Kayla's clit.

She sighed and her head thrashed against Devon's thigh. She angled her face so she could rake her teeth over her friend's skin, telling Devon as clearly as James just had, that she wanted Devon to do it—impale her husband on her tool, so they could watch him unravel as surely as Kayla herself was about to.

Comfort enveloped her. She wasn't the only one about to lose her mind.

Kayla rocked in Neil's hold as Dave picked up the pace and began to really fuck her. He shuttled in and out of her soaked pussy, letting her hold him completely before backing out again and again. Devon moaned as Neil ate her and made her jerk a bit. The forward motion of her hand inserted the lubed vibrator she held through James's muscles and embedded it in his ass. But she didn't stop there.

Devon pushed the toy deeper with a single slow and steady thrust that mimicked Dave's plunge into Kayla. Except, when she had it fully lodged, and Kayla had a detailed view of the action, Devon turned it on with a flick of her thumb.

Kayla jumped when James jerked on top of her. His cock rode her breastbone like it was a greased slip and slide. Neil shuddered beneath her as if James's pleasure was inextricably entwined with his even though they technically weren't even touching. Kayla looked up at Devon, who was grinning down at them. She winked.

The woman was diabolical.

Kayla, and the guys, wholeheartedly approved. A chorus of moans, pants, and groans filled the bedroom. This was familiar and very pleasurable territory. She let her thoughts dissolve and concentrated on the places where her body met those of the people she loved so dearly.

They were okay. They were there with her. And they were making each other feel good.

She still had the most valuable things in her life.

Kayla soaked in ecstasy as if it were a rejuvenating bath, the feel of six male hands roaming over her skin nearly as intoxicating as the two cocks filling her and James working his magic. His mouth pulsed over her clit, sucking in time to the vibrations of the wand in his ass, which was set to his favorite program.

His thighs quivered on either side of her and she knew that he was holding on—holding out—because Dave had commanded him to wait for her. But she wasn't ready to let go and end this cathartic soar through bliss and rapture. Good thing he liked to be tortured.

Neil bucked beneath her, his muscles rippling as he pumped up into her while eating his wife with fervent strokes, which generated the sloppy sounds that characterize all good sex. Devon wasn't unaffected either. Her thigh tensed against Kayla's cheek and her grip on James's toy wavered. The guy wasn't about to let go, though—he rocked back, dragging his tight balls over the pillow of Kayla's chest.

Dave praised them all, encouraging them to keep it up even as he kept fucking, fucking, making Kayla lose track of time and anything except the endorphins flooding her veins. She closed her eyes and went inward, knowing it was selfish and sure that her lovers wouldn't care if she used the sensations they generated to heal herself.

As they fucked, Dave and Neil synced. Before she knew it and definitely before she was ready, her pussy tightened. Her ass strangled Neil's cock, making it harder for him to drill fully inside. And when Dave tapped those tensed muscles inside her, he felt too damn good to resist.

Kayla cried out, trying to warn them of her impending explosion, but James, Neil, Dave, and Devon didn't need any explanation. They were right there, ready to fling themselves over the blazing edge of pleasure with her.

"It's okay, Kayla." Devon stroked her cheek with trembling fingers. "We've got you. We're here with you and it's going to be okay. I promise. Let go, we'll be right by your side."

Kayla's eyes flew open and she saw that Devon was right. Dave was staring down at her with lust, sure, but also affection and a hint of concern that even desire couldn't erase. Neil hugged her from below and James did the same from above.

Her back arched and she shuddered, clamping down hard on Dave and Neil, who fucked her fast, hard, and deep. James ground onto the vibrator in his ass and lapped her clit in the figure eight motion he knew she couldn't resist. Devon threw her head back and swiped her pussy over Neil's mouth, nose, and chin.

Kayla felt strung on the edge of desire for endless moments. When she broke, the world caught up in a flurry of motion, light, and sound. A strangled cry left her throat as she came, flexing and shaking. Doubly so when she felt the guys cave, unable to resist the call of her body to theirs. Dave and Neil flooded her, overflowing her with jet after jet of their warm release.

Devon shrieked, clutching Kayla's shoulder to keep from toppling.

And James joined them, shooting in earthy splats across her belly as he quaked above her.

He was the first to move, sometime later, laving her with gentle licks from the flat of his tongue until she was clean. Kayla kept moving reflexively, rhythmically, which caused Neil to slip from her ass with a groan she echoed. He rolled to his side, tipping her onto the mattress between him and James, then gathered Devon to his chest.

Dave stayed locked within her, talking in gentle tones to her until her body stopped trembling around him. Only then did he pull free, leaving a trail of wetness on her thigh in his wake.

He carefully settled between her and James, squeezing the other man to the side. James didn't seem to mind. He turned to spoon Dave, rubbing her husband's thigh until he huffed out a sigh of relief. Kneeling for that long had cost him, but he hadn't said a word since he'd understood she needed him moving in her, over her.

The five of them snuggled, trying to catch their breath and wallow in the euphoria they'd created and shared with each other.

As bliss gradually receded from Kayla's cells, it left exhaustion behind. She was empty. Freed from agony long enough that she could embrace oblivion and respite from her racing thoughts for a while. Surrounded by people who loved her and would make sure she was protected, she drifted off, sure her problems would be there waiting when she regained consciousness later.

Except now she felt like she would be able to tackle them, one at a time, and wrestle them to the ground.

Nothing stopped the Powertools when they worked together. And they would always have her back.

Kayla nuzzled her face against Dave's chest. When his arms squeezed her tighter, she surrendered to fatigue, sure he wouldn't ever let her go.

None of them would.

4
_____

The next morning, Kayla sat at Devon's kitchen table with her cell phone clutched in her sweaty hand. She stared at the time on the display, each blink of the colon between the 8 and the 59 kicking her in the gut as if it was a tick of the doomsday clock. The instant it flipped over to nine AM, she dialed the number she'd found on the digital copy of her insurance policy the night before. Thank God Dave had uploaded her important documents to the cloud for safe storage. He was pretty much a genius.

Her eyes watered as she thought again of all the other things that had burned up in the fire. Stuff she could never replace, including her wedding dress and photographs from her childhood. They were invaluable to her, but at least getting the insurance company to help replace the things she could and set a plan for rebuilding would be a start.

She tried over and over to remind herself that she wasn't alone and that with help, she could put things back like they were supposed to be.

Except right off the bat, things didn't go as she'd imagined them. Instead of a real person, she got a recording. Not a good omen. "Due to the Westpeak fire, our wait times are currently longer than expected."

"How? It's barely opening time?" Kayla groaned.

She sat through crappy song after crappy song on hold, none of them easing her anxiety in the slightest. Thank God Dave had gone out with James, Neil, and Devon to do a final walkthrough of a flip they'd been wrapping up for the crew or they would realize her calm façade that morning at breakfast had been a sham.

It had been nearly ninety minutes before a man who sounded even more tired than her broke through the soft jazz with a bedraggled, "Hello? Thank you for waiting."

After so long zoned out with that cheesy-ass music droning in the background she nearly dropped her phone in surprise. Wouldn't that have been her luck to hang up by accident?

"Oh! Hi!" How did she even start? How could she explain what had happened without breaking down again.

"Can I help you?" He seemed slightly annoyed or maybe simply frazzled and rushed. She tried to be sympathetic. There were so many other people who had it as bad, or worse, than her. Thankfully no one had been injured at Bare Natural.

"Yes, I am calling because my home and business burned down in the Westpeak fire." There. She'd said it. Gotten it out past the phantom smoke still threatening to choke her as she recalled what they'd seen the day before.

"Was it a total loss?" How could he sound so blasé? This man handled other people's tragedies. At least her life wasn't that miserable. She reaffirmed to herself then that she wanted to help people celebrate their good times, not deal in their misery.

Which was completely unfair. This poor guy was helping people like her. Or at least she hoped he was going to without causing her too much extra grief in the process.

"Yes." Kayla nodded although he couldn't see. It helped her feel better about the raspy whisper she croaked out in response.

"Policy number?" he asked, sort of sounding as if he expected her not to know.

She read it off, clearly enunciating each letter and number.

"Great." He seemed relieved. "You wouldn't believe how many people don't keep that information in a safe place."

"I'll thank my husband for you later." She only realized after she said it how dirty that sounded. "I mean, in a normal, not-kinky kind of way."

And with that the ice was broken.

The agent laughed and so did she. "Sorry, I'm nervous and still freaking out after seeing everything toasted to a crisp. I'm normally a lot more professional, I swear."

She might not have been a lawyer like her brother Gavyn or a doctor like their sister, but she had successfully operated her business for more than a decade, even if she didn't look like the CEO of her life to someone she passed on the street. Normally, she sort of got off on being underestimated, but today...she needed as much help as she could get without any snags.

"I completely understand. I'm sorry for your loss."

And then it hit her. The grief. Because that's what it was. She was mourning the loss of Bare Natural, and their home, and the happy memories that had been wrapped up in those buildings and the woods surrounding them.

She swallowed hard. "Thank you. So you can help me get back on my feet? We think if we could start relaying foundations immediately and finish the framing before winter we might be able to get some interior construction done during the colder months and be ready to open for a mini-season late next summer."

"Oh, uhhh..." He didn't seem to want to ruin their fragile newfound camaraderie. "Ma'am, it could take weeks before we're even able to schedule an appraisal. We need to get clearance from the local authorities to operate in the area and then we arrange the appointments geographically to be most efficient. You'll receive notice about a day in advance when the agent is going to be in your area."

"Weeks?" Kayla calculated how much time was left before the weather would halt construction for the year. And how many working days they could probably squeeze in before even the middle of next season. It wasn't enough, at least not that she could figure. Maybe the Powertools would have some brilliant ideas she couldn't conjure up at the moment. Negativity closed in around her, blocking out her ability to see solutions instead of problem after problem after problem. Things were way worse than she'd thought.

"And after that, it could take another one to two months to process the claim."

"You're kidding, right?" Kayla glared at the phone. And she'd thought they were on the same page.

"Um, no, ma'am."

Ma'am again. Fuck that. Kayla growled.

"And...uh...that's not all." The guy sounded like he

34

might have crawled beneath his desk to hide from her impeding explosion.

"What else?" She didn't know if she could even be mad anymore. She was tired. So tired. And they were just getting started.

"Your policy covers the buildings and the grounds. However, in a disaster like this, if FEMA grants are made —which they likely will be for the Westpeak fire—their emergency funding will cover your belongings. So you'll need to work with them to document all of your possessions and calculate their current replacement value. Then you'll submit that inventory to them and go through their process in tandem with ours. I think you'll find our company to be rather speedy compared to the government."

"Fuck me." Kayla let her forehead clunk onto the table as she tried not to hyperventilate. "Are you telling me that I need to know the make and model of my refrigerator and rugs and all my underwear and shit?"

If I wore underwear, that is.

"Sorry. But yes."

Kayla wasn't the sort to cry easily. She really wasn't. So she pretended the warm trail of liquid making its way down her cheek and onto her neck was rain or a leak in Devon's roof or whatever else it might be other than tears that refused to stay put inside her damn face. Twice in two days was entirely too often for her to be bawling.

"Ma'am? Are you still there?"

"Yeah." She sniffled.

"I can email you the forms you'll need for both processes so you can get started as soon as possible. Again, I'm very sorry this happened to you. Is there anything else I can help you with?"

He didn't say it, but she heard it anyway... *because if not there are a thousand other people like you I need to break shitty news to today.*

"That's it...unless you have a time machine or a magic wand."

"We're fresh out." At least she'd made him laugh again, if only a small chuckle. "Really, I wish there was more I could do."

"Not your fault. Unless you were up here smoking on my mountain, in which case you can go fuck yourself."

The insurance rep actually cracked fully and snorted at that. "I hope you get this sorted out as painlessly as possible. I'm going to email you the documents we discussed. Feel free to shoot me any questions or concerns you have as you're working through this."

"Thanks." Kayla disconnected and sat there, her arms limp at her sides.

They were too heavy to lift and her friends weren't there to do it for her right then.

So she sat there, staring into space, trying to think of workarounds for her new roadblocks until Dave and the rest of the crew returned some time later.

5

Dave tried not to grit his teeth as Kayla tapped her foot on the floor more furiously than a dog scratching an itch. Instead, he laid his hand on her thigh, awed as always by how her powerful frame still didn't take up much of his grip.

"Oh. Sorry. Am I bugging you?" She froze, the tension still winding up her body making him afraid she would snap like a stressed-out spring.

"No. Not exactly. I just don't know how to help and it's making me feel useless." Dave leaned in and kissed her cheek, trying to soften his admission.

"Useless. Yeah, that's exactly how I feel." Kayla dropped her head on his shoulder and collapsed against him, thankfully sure that he would catch her, which—of course—he did.

From the other side of the counter where he was pouring himself a cup of coffee, James asked, "How much longer did they say it would be before an appraiser could make it out here?"

"Not anytime soon." She groaned. "They're going to let me know when this region is next on the list."

"That means like, what, a day's notice or something? More than just five minutes, right?" James asked, and Dave immediately knew what he was getting at because he had the same idea.

"Look, if we're not getting anything done here...." Devon glanced from her guys to Kayla and Dave. "And you'll have enough warning that we can come back in time for any appointments...why don't we go to Middletown so we can help Joe and Mike out?"

Devon didn't say it, but the work Mike and Joe were doing was funding this half of the crew's time off to come to her aide. While that was incredibly generous, it would be better to contribute while they could now and use those reserves when Kayla needed them to be actively working on the rebuild.

Dave looked at Kayla and shrugged. "It'll help pass the time, and swinging a hammer is good for venting frustration. You can come on site with us if you want, or hang out with Kate and Morgan. Help them with... whatever it is they're doing or work on the inventory bullshit you need to do for the government or maybe spend some quality time with Gavyn and Noah. And in the evenings, we can draw up plans for Bare Natural 2.0 with input from the full crew instead of just us."

He held his breath as he waited for her reaction. These past several days she had been on edge, not at all the calm, unflappable, ultimately happy woman he'd loved pretty much forever. Would she think he was betraying her if he admitted he craved action instead of this never-ending spinning of their wheels?

Hell, it wasn't often he saw Devon of all people

walking on eggshells around Kayla. But none of them wanted to risk wounding her more than she'd already been lately. Or setting her off. She wasn't herself. And he didn't know how to do more than put a Band-Aid on the problem, taking her mind off things for the duration of a favorite TV show, or a quickie in the shower, or long enough to feed her a warm meal. Was this how impotent she'd felt after his accident?

His stomach lurched, making him glad he hadn't yet partaken of the bacon and eggs James was whipping up for them. Kayla had stood by him—hell, *for* him—when he couldn't do it himself, and now Dave had to do the same for her.

Would she see their suggestion as an abandonment or as a way to help her snap out of this funk that was so unlike her to fall into, which was what he intended it to be?

Kayla stared at the four of them and their very carefully composed faces as they prepared to duck for cover if necessary. Then she surprised them by bursting out laughing. "Are you that afraid of me? Jeez. I must need a vacation. Get me some coffee and breakfast and let's hit the road. You're right: we might as well be productive. And...being together, with the whole crew, will be good for me too. I'm sorry I've been such a pain in your asses."

"Yas!" James fist-pumped even as Neil was taking his phone from his back pocket to text the good news to the rest of the crew in their ongoing group chat. "I mean, you haven't been any trouble, but it sucks not being able to do more from here. I think it'll be good to get out of here and really think things through without constantly having to face the aftermath of the fire."

They couldn't so much as drive down the street

without seeing people who'd been displaced bunking up with friends, signs for still-missing pets, and advertisements for cleanup crews staked into the corners at intersections. It was impossible to escape the far-reaching ramifications unless they hunkered down inside. And hiding out was starting to make Dave stir-crazy.

The rest of their little gang, too.

"You better make double." Neil got the eggs out of the refrigerator for his husband. "I have a feeling we're going to need our energy when we get there. And I'm not talking about working the Hot Rods construction site either."

"We did leave in kind of a hurry, and things have been so tense since then. I bet you're right. Someone is going to crack pretty quick, probably me, and need to blow off steam together." Kayla sighed. "Sorry about that. About everything."

"It's not your fault." Devon crossed to her and wormed between Dave and Kayla. "I know this is the last thing you ever would have wanted. I'm sorry we can't snap our fingers and make things right as fast as they were destroyed."

"I guess that's just not how life works. Progress is slow and steady, but tragedy can wipe away years of hard work and doing the right thing in an instant." Kayla's smile faded a bit. "We should make the best of the situation, though. Isn't that what we've always done?"

"Yup." Dave rubbed the scars on his thigh, then held his hand out to Kayla. "We're going to get through this. It might take a while and it won't always be easy, but we can do it. Being with the rest of the crew will only make the time go faster. We were going to be missing them so hard this summer and now we have a chance to go be with them. We should take it while we can."

"I'm grateful that I have you." Kayla hugged Devon, then leaned in to kiss Dave. "All of you. All right. Let's go."

6

Dave tried not to check on Kayla for the four-thousandth time during their drive, and failed. He glanced over, or attempted to, but it was like she could feel his stare. Every time, she turned her head to meet his gaze.

"I swear, I'm fine." She squeezed his hand where their fingers were entwined.

"It's okay if you're not," he told her again.

"No one's expecting you to have it together right now," James added from the front passenger's seat. "If you can't tell us when you're struggling, who are you going to admit it to?"

"Okay, fair enough." Kayla sighed. "I'm a hot mess. But I feel better heading out here. You were right. It's better to go somewhere we can actually do something and be around the rest of the crew. Counting the seconds waiting for something to happen back home was driving me nuts."

"Me too." Devon peeked into the rearview mirror,

taking her eyes off the road only long enough to flash them a grin.

"Morgan said she and Devra made us an awesome picnic lunch. Joe and Mike gave their imposter crew the afternoon off so we can goof around." Neil did a fist pump from the other side of Kayla.

Dave snorted. "Don't let the guys working on the Hot Rods expansion hear you call them the *imposter crew*."

"Yeah, we need to get used to the fact that we're not going to be Mike and Joe's crew members anymore. We've been replaced by younger, studlier people." James turned and stared out the window, not as amused as the rest of them.

Dave narrowed his eyes, hoping that wasn't going to be an issue. He glanced over at Neil, who shrugged, but even he wasn't as jovial as usual.

Life was messy lately, that was for sure.

Kayla seemed to sense the tension, too. She patted Neil's knee and leaned her head on his shoulder. They rode in relative quiet the rest of the trip, the radio keeping them company as the miles rolled past.

But as soon as they pulled into the parking lot of the Hot Rods garage, everyone perked up. It would be impossible not to be excited when friends began streaming from the open bays, Tom and Ms. Brown's cabin behind it, and the construction site where Mike and Joe were overseeing the expansion of the mechanics' home base.

Dave squeezed himself out of the van, hopping a bit as his bad leg protested being cramped up for hours. Kayla slid beside him and wrapped her arm around his waist instinctively. He did the same to her, both of them stronger when they had each other to lean on.

Bryce was the first one to reach them, his dog Buster McHightops close behind. He was one of the few people who made Dave feel normal-sized instead of some overgrown hulk. Especially when he crouched down, wincing at the zing in his thigh in order to ruffle Buster's ears. They'd once been as black as his owner's hair but now were streaked through with gray. He could relate. "Hey, old man, how are you?"

"Don't be insulting my husband like that," teased Kaelyn, Bryce's wife, as she joined them.

"Oof. Thanks a lot." Bryce was laughing, though, when he turned and grabbed her around her middle, swinging her in circles and tickling her until she cracked up.

Behind Bryce and Kaelyn, a mini-Bryce emerged with a wriggly puppy in his arms. Buster was doing his best to live forever, but it was clear the family was having him train his legacy. "Hi, Mr. Dave! Have you met my puppy yet? Professor Puddinpop is brothers with Nathan's puppy. Isn't that cool?"

Dave's heart gave a happy lurch at the mention of Joe's son, who carried his DNA. He and Kayla had decided they loved spoiling their friends' kids and sending them home more than having their own, but he wouldn't lie— knowing he'd passed on a bit of himself to someone else had always given him a bit of a warm glow. Especially since he'd been able to help Joe and Morgan achieve their dream of being parents.

"Professor Puddinpop? Did your dad help you pick that out or does excellent taste in dog names run in the family?" Dave chuckled as he petted Jett's very excited little pup too.

"He came up with that all on his own." Kaelyn beamed at their son, then held her hand out to their daughter, who had an awful lot of her mom's strength and determination for a kid who was only four or five.

"Mom says our next pet can be a cat and *I* get to pick its name." Kinze held her arms up and Kaelyn scooped her into her embrace and nodded, reinforcing her promise, not that she'd get away with anything less at this point.

"Why don't you take Buster and the Professor behind the garage and let them play?" Bryce pointed the kids toward the backyard, where Sabra and Holden's twins were climbing a tree with Nola and Nova's girls and Mike and Joe's kids. They were getting to be their own little clan.

"Okay. Byeeeeeeeeeeee!" Jett shouted as he took off running, Kinze skipping along after him.

Dave clasped Bryce's extended hand and used the connection to lever himself back to his feet. "Thanks."

"No problem. Good to see you all again." He used the hold to draw Dave into a one-armed man-clinch, then traded him for Kayla, who he enfolded in a bear hug. "I'm so sorry to hear about the resort. You know we're here if there's anything we can do."

"We appreciate that." Kayla smothered him back, making Dave only slightly jealous if it did prove they were better off surrounded by people who cared. "For now, I could use some distractions."

"We have *plenty* of those around here." Ms. Brown, Nola and Amber's mom, and Uncle Tom, Ms. Brown's husband—who was also the father of the Hot Rods garage owner, Eli—had emerged from their house to welcome the rest of the crew back to Middletown.

Dave had to admit that the more they did this, the more it started to feel like coming home.

He shook his head, erasing the thought. Their home was back at Bare Natural, or it would be again once it was rebuilt.

Then the trickle of people turned into a full-on crowd, the rest of the Hot Rods mechanics being joined by Mike and Joe from the construction site and their wives, Morgan and Kate.

The fresh air seemed to be agreeing with them. Kate was glowing, maybe also because she was pregnant, and Morgan seemed to have an extra bounce in her step. After plodding along for nearly a week, just seeing them refreshed Dave. A little alone time with them would go even further to rejuvenating him and, he hoped, Kayla.

Kayla ran to meet her friends and they hung on to each other, telling her again how sorry they were for the fire. Dave would be grateful never to hear of the damn thing again, but he was glad to see his wife looking more like her usual self already.

"Well, I hear Morgan and several of the other kids planned a special lunch for you all, so we'll let you enjoy it. Come and see us before you head out after, okay?" Tom squeezed Dave's shoulders, probably referring to the Hot Rods and Hot Rides rather than their children, then he and Ms. Brown stepped back, retreating toward their house. How they managed the perfect blend of supportive and maintaining their distance, Dave wasn't sure, but it had been a while since he'd been the recipient of that kind of parental concern and he couldn't say he minded in the least.

"We will. See you later." He waved, then did the same to the Hot Rods, who needed to get back to work if he was going by the number of sexy cars lined up outside the bays.

"Yeah, come on." Joe tried to act casual, except the high set of his shoulders gave him away. Had he been looking forward to this all day? Hopefully, Kayla could relax enough to enjoy whatever they had planned and not hurt their feelings by accident. Though, he was sure they'd understand if that wasn't the case. Unless...was there something more than lunch at stake? "I want to take a walk down by the lake. We set up a picnic there. It's the stretch of land Uncle Tom is thinking of selling. To us. For a house. You know, if we decide to stay."

Ah, so that was the catch. In his heart, Dave knew it was already a done deal. Joe wasn't coming back. And as much as it hurt to know they wouldn't be as close as before, he couldn't muster anything but joy for his friend, who obviously was finding his way forward both in his career and his personal life.

Being left behind didn't sit especially well with Dave, but he'd come to grips with it eventually...he hoped. For right now, he needed to focus on Kayla and make her his priority.

Dave, Neil, James, Devon, and Kayla joined Mike, Kate, Joe, and Morgan, all of them falling easily into their usual conversations and teasing. As they walked they split off into pairs or small groupings that were ever-morphing, each of them utterly comfortable with all the others.

Kayla drew a deep breath then let it out in a whoosh, her hand slipping into Dave's while they strolled through the forest toward the lake. As they approached, he could feel the welcome coolness. He mirrored his wife, drawing the fresh scent of earth and leaves and water into his lungs. It reminded him of home in a way, but better because this land was like their mountain had been before the blaze. Before everything had been annihilated.

It was so much more refreshing than the acrid smell of seared earth.

This last burst of summer, the final hot days when the foliage had already started to dry out and turn golden in places, was usually peak season at their resort. It had been years since he'd had time between helping Kayla with check-ins and turnovers on top of his own job on the crew to really savor the nature that had drawn them to that spot, one not so different than the place they were enjoying with their friends now.

When they reached the lakefront, Kayla gasped. The light of the early afternoon sun reflected off the surface of the water, making it sparkle and dance.

Someone had stacked hay bales and covered them with a white-and-red checked tablecloth then used others to form bench seats. Sunflowers in mason jars stood in for centerpieces. Instantly, Dave was hit with a wave of nostalgia.

It reminded him of the time he, Mike, Kate, Neil, and James had helped Joe set up his first date with Morgan, which seemed to have gone pretty damn well and started them down the path to this present where they were still going strong together.

In the background a flat area wide enough for several buildings stretched before the trees picked up again. Wildflowers blossomed in a multicolored blanket that swayed in the breeze.

"What do you think?" Joe asked.

"It's...incredible." Kayla breathed out a sigh. "The picnic of course, but the site. Wow."

"Could you see us building a house here on the shore? Or maybe two, if Mike and Kate are going to stay a while..." He rushed past that possibility before uneasiness could take up residence in Dave's gut again. "...you know, we could always sell them after. Another portfolio-builder and investment for Powertools if and when they go back home."

The thing about Joe was that he talked more when he was nervous. Usually quiet and steady, he didn't often go this route. Before Dave could reassure him that anyone would fall in love with this place and that he didn't blame the guy for doing so, Kayla jumped in.

"Hell, I could see building a whole resort here." She swung her arm out wide. This front section would be perfect for a day spa and lodge with cabins nestled in the woods along a winding path back there that would afford people privacy."

After all, most of their guests chose not to wear clothes most of the time.

She shook herself. "I mean. It would be perfect if that's what you were thinking of. I can see a house or two here too. It would be lovely. So relaxing."

Devon was nodding and so were James and Neil, as if they could envision it.

A chill ran down Dave's spine despite the abnormal warmth of the day. It was like he'd had a premonition or some glimpse of the future. This was where his friends would live. He knew it.

Now he just had to accept it.

"You okay?" Kayla turned to him and squeezed his fingers, drawing him back into the moment. It was a gorgeous day, all the people he loved—including the Powertools kids—were taken care of, the crew was together, and they were damn well going to enjoy it.

"Great." He strolled with her to the makeshift table and admired Morgan's hard work. Even better was when he sampled some of every dish she and Devra had whipped up and had some gooey chocolate dessert thing Morgan had baked just for them to look forward to at the end.

Neil let out a huge belch that practically reverberated through the valley.

"Gross." James shoved him and Neil flipped backward off the hay into a slightly squishy patch of dirt and mud. Devon cracked up at their antics.

Neil lunged toward her with a grin. "Think that's funny, huh?"

She squealed as he tugged her down and wrestled in the thick mud with her. Somehow, she ended up straddling him, her arms braced on his shoulders.

Dave sat up straighter, paying close attention to the vibe, which promised to become even hotter than the sun overhead.

Mike leaned forward and casually said, "You'd better wash that off before you go back to Tom and Ms. Brown's house. Wouldn't want to get anything dirty."

Before he'd even finished his not-so-subtle order, they were stripping off their clothes, dashing for the lake. Dave looked to Kayla and winked. "Guess we better go play lifeguard. Wouldn't want anyone to drown."

"Very responsible of you, husband of mine." Kayla never had to be encouraged to shed her clothing. In fact, he was kind of shocked she'd left her T-shirt and jeans on that long. Her naked form dazzled him more than the beauty of the landscape. She held her hand out to him.

He got naked then joined her as the rest of the crew followed suit.

Joe bolted past them to belly flop into the water yelling, "Skinnydipping! Yahoo!"

7
_____

Dave crashed into the lake, relieved when floating took some of the pressure off his leg. Riding in the car for hours without stretching the damn thing out was never a good idea. Follow that up with a trek on an uneven, sloped path, then sitting on a low bench, and he was just about done. But for Kayla, he would do it a thousand times over.

Besides, if he asked later, she'd give him one of her incredible massages, he was sure of it.

"Last man to the swim platform has to blow me!" Mike shouted as he kicked off his shoes then dove into the crystal waters as the women cracked up and waded in behind them, rolling their eyes and talking shit about their antics.

The five men cut through his wake, their arms chopping the surface and flinging droplets all over the place. If James didn't seem to be trying as hard as the rest of them, it was probably because going down on Mike was more of a reward than a punishment for him.

Dave passed James and kept going, overtaking Neil and then Joe with consistent strokes of his arms. He'd nearly caught even Mike by the time they reached the wooden rectangle, the size of maybe six pallets stuck together, and climbed onto it.

He flopped onto his back, breathing hard, and let the sun chase away the chill brought on by the refreshing dip. Propped up on his elbows, he watched the rest of the crew and then the women behind them approaching at a more civilized pace, laughing and talking as they paddled out. Kayla floated on her back, lazily stroking her way toward him, her breasts on display, the piercings in her nipples glinting in the sunlight. He couldn't help it—his dick twitched and started to swell.

As predicted, James reached them dead last, with a wicked smile on his face.

"You could have made it look close, at least." Neil snorted as he boosted his husband onto the platform next to Dave. The smaller guy shrugged and turned to Mike, who'd settled onto the single beat-up lounge chair on the platform, reclining in it like a king—or their foreman, which he definitely was and always would be no matter what their official job titles were.

Dave noticed he wasn't the only one who apparently liked the idea of an afternoon spent together crew-style. Joe shoved himself onto the boards, then reached behind him to extend his hand to Morgan. His cock was hanging heavy between his legs, more than half hard already.

Kate perched on the arm of Mike's chair, leaning back so that she was cradled on his upper chest. Her spot left plenty of room for James to crawl between Mike's legs. He wasted no time taking Mike's cock into his mouth and starting to suck.

"Fuck," Mike groaned. He gripped the arm of the chair on one side while he clutched his wife's waist with his other hand. "Your mouth feels like it's roasting me after that water."

James pulled off long enough to ask, "Does that mean you want me to stop?"

"Hell no." Mike growled and thrust his hips upward.

Neil and Devon floated in the water, their arms crossed on the platform and their chins resting on their arms as they watched their husband enjoy his dessert. Devon mock-scolded him. "Don't you dare try to get out of it now. You can't come back over here and play with us until Mike says you've done a good job."

Neil cocked a brow, then leaned over to kiss her. "How about me? I'm not sure I can wait much longer if you keep being bossy like that."

Devon grinned and said, "Well, I'd go down on you if it wouldn't mean drowning."

Neil was out of the water in a flash, turning so that he sat on the edge of the platform, his feet dangling in the water. He reached out and took Devon's upper arm in his hand, then used the grip to guide her between his legs. He spread them and said, "I've got something you can hang onto."

"Careful you don't get splinters in anything important." Devon chuckled as Dave groaned and clutched his own balls in sympathy. She looped her arms around Neil's waist and buried her face between his legs.

While Dave couldn't see through her head, he didn't have to in order to guess what she was doing. The way Neil's eyes rolled back before he clutched at her shoulder and speared his fingers into her short hair told Dave everything he needed to know.

And that was even before he unleashed a long, loud groan.

James worked Mike while Devon did the same to Neil, which had Dave antsy for some attention of his own. But the throbbing in his leg made him sure he was going to have to choose his next move carefully. While Kayla didn't mind riding him most times, since the fire she'd seemed to prefer him taking the lead and he wasn't about to disappoint her or drag her out of this rejuvenating moment.

This was exactly why they'd come.

So he bent over and clasped her wrists, then hauled her from the lake, water sluicing from her perfect-to-him body in crystalline rivulets. He took his time kissing her, wrapping her in his arms to make sure she wasn't cold. Her wet body plastered to his guaranteed he wasn't anything of the sort. And when she pulled back and smiled up at him, ready for more, he guided her down to her back on the platform and followed right behind.

Dave knelt on the uneven wood surface, which wobbled in the water, and winced. "Fuck this. I have a better idea."

Thank the stars he'd focused on building up strength in his arms for times, just like this, when his leg could have otherwise been a hindrance. He positioned Kayla with her ass teetering on the edge and her body parallel to Neil and Devon.

She peeked over at them while Dave turned and, with a single fluid motion, stepped off the platform again, going under with a whoosh that rang in his ears. When he surfaced next to Devon, he apologized for the waves that made her slosh in between Neil's legs. But once he ensured she was steady again, he beached himself over Kayla, probably looking like a hairy whale at an aquarium show and not caring much about his tanned ass on display. After running a naturist resort for more than a decade, there wasn't much of him not used to being exposed to daylight.

Unfortunately, the cold hit him like a delayed fist in the gut. He shook water from his hair and hooted. "That's a bit chilly."

"Didn't think your plan through all the way, did you?" Mike chuckled as his hand on James's head directed the other man up and down, up and down. "Don't worry, I'm sure Neil or James will be more than happy to fuck your wife for you."

Oh hell no. Not this time. He braced himself on his bulging forearms and admired his wife beneath him. She was so pretty, her tattoos bright in the late summer sun.

Kayla immediately wrapped her thighs around his waist, hugging him tight and bringing him close to exactly where he wanted to be most.

He levered himself more upright, part in the water and part out, using the buoyancy to help offset his weight and keep from crushing her. "Much better."

His wife smiled up at him and hummed. "I think so too, but it'll be best if you get inside me. Hurry. I'll warm you right up again."

He wasn't about to keep her waiting.

He braced himself on straight-locked arms, his legs floating behind him. Propping himself up with his arms was no problem and the weight off his thigh and knee was a relief, allowing him to focus on entirely more pleasurable parts of his body.

Kayla glanced over and shared a secret smile with Devon, who clenched her fingers on Neil's flanks, ignoring everything but making him moan into the afternoon air.

Dave fisted his cock and pumped it a few times, his balls bobbing in the water and only increasing how ridiculously good he felt. He couldn't wait to bury himself in his wife's steamy pussy and show her exactly how much he loved seeing this hint of the old her instead of the one he'd feared would be irreparably damaged, scarred emotionally like he had been physically.

He balanced on one forearm and hunched his back as he ringed the base of his cock with two fingers and aimed it at the opening to Kayla's body. She arched her back and squirmed until they were aligned, fit together perfectly. Her head went back and her eyes opened so wide he could see the sky reflected in them as he set the head of his cock against her flesh and began to work inside it.

She scalded him, feeling even warmer and softer than usual as he joined himself to her.

It took longer and involved a few more grunts and adjustments as he used his grip to drag the rest of his body closer to her, but each inch he burrowed inside Kayla made them both moan and sigh. She stretched around his erection, taking him gracefully despite his unusual size. And yet her pussy rippled around him, with velvety heat.

She squeezed him, her muscles working around his shaft as he began to bore in and out.

Kayla's arms went around him. She caressed his back as she smiled up at him. "Hi."

"Hey." He laughed, then said, "Sorry I skipped straight to the good stuff."

"I couldn't wait either." She shifted beneath him, helping him grind into her.

Dave ducked his head and kissed Kayla while he made love to her, wishing he'd taken more time to toy with her piercings and taste the fresh water on her skin.

"You can feel free to hurry the fuck up too," Morgan teased Joe.

He lay down next to Neil and patted his abs. "I'm not going to argue with you—I'm not that dumb. Hop on, cupcake."

She did just that, sinking over him in a crouch that would have made a stripper jealous. Reaching behind her, she angled his dick upward and slid onto it as if she'd been waiting years instead of probably only a few hours to have him inside her again.

Dave didn't blame her. Joe was a hell of a fuck. His cock jerked as he thought of the times his friend had bent him over on a job site and sated him until he went home to Kayla.

As if she could read his thoughts, she whispered in his ear, "Maybe next time he'll fuck you while you fuck me. Would you like that?"

Dave groaned and drilled into her, harder than he'd intended. She didn't seem to mind, her pussy squeezing him and making it impossible for him to slip free. Neil was staring at him fucking Kayla while Devon worked his cock with her mouth.

And soon Kate was clearing her throat. "I think you've done a good enough job there, James. Mind if I steal that cock from you? I think Devon might have a use for your talents."

Devon raised her head long enough to shout, "Yup! Uh huh. I do."

James raised his head and looked to Mike, who nodded. "Debt paid. Thanks."

Before James could stand, Mike wrapped his hand around the back of James's neck and used the grip to haul him upward. He showed proper appreciation with one hell of a kiss. Kate stroked both of their cheeks as she smiled lovingly at them.

And then, when they broke apart, she rubbed both of their cocks too. James shuddered.

"Better get in that water so you last until your wife does." Mike nudged him toward the edge of the platform. "Or help her get there faster—that's even better."

When they did this, fucking in front of each other but staying within their married units, they almost always seemed to come at the same time or close to it. Dave thought it was like their bodies' way of being demonstrated they were united, even when they were technically separate.

He couldn't say they tried to do it on purpose, but their connection was so strong that when one of them felt something deeply, it affected the rest of them equally.

Mike grabbed Kate and flipped her, gently since he'd never risk hurting their baby, but quickly so that she ended up on the fully reclined chair beneath him. Dave couldn't help but remember when they'd fucked on a similar one beside the pool at the renovation job where they'd met Kate, who lived next door.

That summer had changed his life forever. For the better.

James leapt between Neil and Dave, diving into the water in a graceful arc then bobbing to the surface between his wife's legs. He wrapped his arms around her waist and treaded water, but no matter how he angled his head, he couldn't quite fasten his mouth to her pussy without choking a bit on the lake.

"Hang on, let me help." Neil tipped forward and wrapped his hands around Devon's tiny waist, then leaned back again, effectively cantilevering her ass up and out of the water.

"Perfect." James smacked it playfully, then slipped beneath her, lapping at her even as he slid three fingers into her pussy.

She moaned around Neil, who tensed, but he never wavered or let her dip even a fraction of an inch.

By now they were all lost to the pleasure they inspired in each other. The sights and sounds of his best friends experiencing as much bliss as Dave was only torqued his enjoyment higher. Kayla began to meet him halfway, her hips rocking upward as he plunged down so that he bottomed out in her on every pass.

Her nipples were tight, thrusting her jewelry into the afternoon air. They shook as he rode her harder and faster, and he knew she got off on it because her hand slipped from his back to tug on them.

Mike wasn't wasting any time either. He was threatening to break the poor weathered chair with his steady thrusts into Kate. The last time she'd been pregnant there had been periods where she wasn't interested in sex. That certainly wasn't an issue now. Her nails raked Mike's back, urging him to screw her harder. And he did.

Water sloshed around the platform as they caused it to rock. But soon Dave couldn't hear the splashes anymore over the moans and gritty curses that burst from each of them on occasion. Morgan rode Joe as if she were a world-class cowgirl instead of a baker, and both Devon and James sucked and fingered their lovers while James's hand stroked his cock beneath the surface of the lake. Dave peered down at Kayla and saw her eyes glaze over, as entranced as he was by the energy they generated when they shared their most intimate moments like this.

It made his balls draw tight to his body and his cock lurch inside her.

But before he could take a break or shout a warning, Kate shrieked, "I can't stop it! I can't. Need it. Now. Sorry."

There was nothing to apologize for. Dave would tell her so as soon as he could breathe again. Because he was right there with her, and apparently so was everyone else.

Devon moaned and Neil slapped his palm on the platform. His ass clenched and relaxed in time to the grunts that made Dave sure he was pumping his release down his wife's throat. Morgan arched in Joe's hold and shuddered on top of him, her orgasm drawing Joe's come straight from his balls.

Dave looked over just long enough to see a drop or two squeeze out of her and slide down Joe's dick before he lost it. He crushed his lips to Kayla's precisely as she unraveled around him and he began to gush deep inside her.

Mike caved last, as if he'd waited a second or two longer than the rest of his crew members, to make sure they were sated before he joined them, before emptying himself into his wife.

It felt so fucking good to be there with the Powertools, especially after such a stressful couple of days, that Dave's orgasm kept wringing him dry long after he should have been spent.

It was more than a physical release. His climax filled in some of the fractures in his soul and shored up the confidence that had eroded every time he'd glimpsed the desperation in Kayla's eyes lately. And there was none of it there at the moment. Instead, she was flying, staring up at him with awe and surrender not unlike his own.

They hung there together as one heartbeat stretched into a hundred or two and then the magic began to dissipate, or at least to turn from something intense to something enduring that forged this lifelong bond between them.

Joe pulled out of Morgan with a sigh. He laid her down gently, then flopped onto his side next to her...or would have if he hadn't been closer to the edge than he'd realized. He rolled right off the swim platform and into the lake with a plop and splash worthy of a slab of iceberg shearing off into the ocean.

Dave laughed so loud he swore he startled birds from the trees on the bank furthest from them. And even better, so did Kayla. It eased his heart so much to hear his wife cracking up that he held her even closer to his chest than he had before.

Joe surfaced, shaking his head. A cone of water ringed his head like a distorted halo, making him look half man and half dog. "Funny, huh?"

He reached up and snagged Mike's ankle, using his grip to yank the other blissed out guy into the lake too. And soon it was a full-on aquatic fight.

Dave kissed Kayla's cheek, then unwound himself from her and stood so that he could lumber toward the edge and cannonball—even if one leg was tucked tighter to his chest than the other—into the cool, refreshing water. The splash rained down on the women on the platform, who shrieked and laughed as they snuggled up together.

He wondered what it would be like if they could simply erase the big black mark the destruction of Bare Natural had left on their souls and start over. Maybe somewhere exactly like this.

8

Kayla looked out the window and bit her lip as Morgan drove her from the house they were renting over to Hot Rides, the motorcycle sister-shop of Hot Rods. It just so happened to be owned by Kayla's brother, Gavyn.

"Are you nervous or something?" Morgan shot her a glance out of the corner of her eye before returning her focus to the winding forest road. Kayla stopped tapping her fingers around the door handle.

"I mean, kind of?" She wasn't sure what exactly to call the complicated ball of feelings that overtook her every time she dealt with her family. It wasn't like she'd ever really fit in with her ultra-successful and very traditional siblings and parents. But a whole lot of distance had been jammed between them as they sank deeper into their own lives and routines. "I guess things have been tense for a while now. You know how it is. Gav's got his own life here now, and it's so...*different*...from before."

"Better, you mean?" Morgan asked. "Because he's sober and doing something he loves instead of working a job that makes him miserable just for the sake of earning a living?"

Kayla shrugged. If she were a good sister, that's what she would mean. "I'm glad he's out of the divorce business, yes. And of course I'm thrilled he's gotten his shit together and is actively managing his addiction. Yeah, all that."

"But..." Morgan waited with the patience only a parent could have developed.

"Is it wrong that I'm still afraid of trusting him completely?" Kayla hated that she even thought something so disloyal. "Things aren't like they were before —when we were kids, or even ten years ago. He was the only relative who ever fully accepted me, and then..."

"He let you down." Morgan sighed. "I know how much he hurt you. It's not unreasonable to want to guard your heart."

"It's been years. I need to get over it. It wasn't like he did something malicious to attack me personally." Kayla toyed with the piercing in her lip. "If Amber can forgive him, I need to too. All the way. It's just—we never really closed that loop fully and now it's kind of awkward, always hanging there in the space between us, you know?"

"Well, if you're going to be spending some time here, maybe it's best to have a conversation or two with him and get this bullshit sorted out." Morgan smiled sadly at Kayla. "Especially now, you could really use your brother. Don't let old shit fester between you and keep you from a meaningful relationship with someone you love."

Kayla nodded. "You're right. I'll talk to him. It's just a lot on top of everything else right now."

She thought of the spreadsheets she'd abandoned when Morgan asked if she wanted to take a ride over there with her. Dozens of hours and tons of research, and she felt like she'd hardly begun the inventory of Bare Natural, never mind her and Dave's house or the lodge. And that was only the first tiny step toward rebuilding.

Ugh.

They turned into the Hot Rides driveway, rolling past the flaming motorcycle sign Sally had painted for the shop. Whether or not they had the best relationship, Kayla was proud of her brother and how he'd built something from nothing. Sort of like she had at Bare Natural. And twice as much because he'd done it while overcoming something as difficult as alcoholism and starting a family with Amber and their new son Noah at the same time. She wasn't sure she was half as strong as him now that she was being tested too. Maybe it was time she told him so.

He might be her big brother, but that didn't mean she couldn't man up.

Kayla wiped her palms on her ripped jeans, then climbed from the car as Morgan did the same. Over the roof, her friend asked, "Do you want me to go with you?"

"Nah, I'm good. Devra is waiting for you to test out those new recipes." Kayla grinned. "Make sure you bring me samples so I can give my very valuable opinion on them."

"You just want snacks." Morgan laughed.

"Damn straight. Thanks." Kayla waved. She angled toward the garage while Morgan headed down the path toward Devra, Trevon, and Quinn's tiny home in the cluster of houses where the Hot Rides mechanic family lived when they weren't working together.

What would it be like if the Powertools had an arrangement like that? For years, they'd had their own spaces, but the unofficial gathering place had been her and Dave's home, in the seclusion of the woods, where they wouldn't be bothered by nosy neighbors and their judgmental looks. With Mike and Joe spending most of their time in Middletown for the foreseeable future and her and Dave staying at Devon, James, and Neil's place, things were in upheaval.

Whatever they did next, they should maybe take a lesson from the Hot Rides and Hot Rods gangs. No reason they couldn't make some improvements instead of putting things back exactly as they had been before. She would mention it to Devon, Neil, and James later. Maybe there was a home for sale in their neighborhood, or perhaps the trio would consider moving out to Bare Natural.

Kayla looked around as she strolled through the open garage bay. There were motorcycles in various stages of repair, from parts scattered on a workbench to a mostly complete frame on Wren's welding station to polished beauties that looked like they were in for routine maintenance.

In one corner, Ransom and Levi huddled over a restoration piece with Sevan, Joy's little sister. She wore grease-smeared jean cut-offs with a wrench tucked in her back pocket and looked happier than Kayla had ever seen her before. She'd come on full time at the shop, and Gavyn had raved about her increasing their productivity. Plus, to be honest, some of their customers seemed to really enjoy Wren and Sevan working on their bikes. They were like one of those sexy motorcycle calendars come to life, with the bonus of being as capable as they were beautiful.

Ransom and Levi hung out at the shop sometimes, but Kayla knew they were also working for Wren's husband

Jordan and would sometimes disappear for a while, assigned to whatever secret op the guy had been tagged in by various government agencies or private clients who needed extra security. No one asked very many questions about that, so she followed suit, respecting what they did even if she didn't know the details.

"Hey, Kayla!" Sevan set her socket on the drop cloth protecting the garage floor as soon as she caught sight of her entering. She rushed over and extended her arms. "I'm so sorry to hear about the fire."

Sevan stopped short, though, glancing down at her soiled clothes. Kayla wasn't about to let a bit of dirt stop her from accepting a much-needed hug. These days she could use all of them she could get.

She leaned into the other woman's embrace, glad she had when Sevan seemed relieved. The young woman hadn't had it easy either. Maybe it was important, and novel, for her to be accepted too. Kayla figured you never could go wrong with a hug. Behind Sevan, Ransom and Levi were shooting them a mix of relieved and worried glances.

"It's okay, guys. I'm not going to burst into tears. Not at the moment anyway." Kayla embraced the two big guys as enthusiastically as she had their girlfriend. She took their semi-awkwardness as a personal challenge. Ransom had done hard time and Levi, well...he could use some thawing too. She made it her mission to hand out cuddles like candy at Halloween from then on. "You're safe."

"Good to know." Ransom looked so relieved she couldn't help but chuckle.

"Is there something we can do for you?" Sevan wondered. "Anything at all?"

"Nah, I'm good. The Powertools are helping out. Mike

and Joe are here working on the Hot Rods expansion, obviously, and they're in talks with one of the guys Kason introduced them to at Ollie, Van, and Kyra's wedding about a major build in town. That's taking a lot of the financial pressure off their business so Dave, James, Neil, and Devon can help me restore Bare Natural. Or at least that's the plan, once the red tape eventually gets cleared up." She rubbed her throbbing temple as the pile of bullshit she needed to wade through flashed into her mind. "Anyway, I stopped by to talk to my brother, if he's not too busy."

She peeked around, through the glass door that led into the office but didn't see him inside.

"Oh, shit. Sorry." Levi grimaced. "He went to a meeting at a private client's house. Another one of Kason's buddies, a couple hours away. Didn't he tell you?"

Kayla frowned. Of course they'd assume she and Gavyn spoke more than they did. It was kind of embarrassing to admit they knew her own brother far better than she felt like she did these days. "No, I should have texted. We came up kind of spur of the moment yesterday after we found out there's going to be a wait for the insurance to come through, so I just stopped over. I should have checked."

Awkward.

Sevan glanced over at Ransom and Levi. Whatever kind of stare she shot them, they seemed to understand. They backed off and made like they were busy fussing over the component Sevan had probably already fixed perfectly.

Their girl took Kayla's elbow in her firm grip and steered her toward the outside. They leaned together against the external wall of the garage, Kayla looking over at the handsome house Gavyn shared with his wife, Amber, and their baby son, Noah.

"You know, we have more in common than you might think." Sevan cleared her throat. "My sister, Joy, was the legitimate daughter in our family. I was the dirty little secret. I know what it's like to be the black sheep. Not that I think you are, but I can see you feel some kind of way about your brother and your place here."

Kayla didn't bother to deny it. Sevan was pretty cool. If she ended up spending more time in Middletown now that Mike, Kate, Joe, and Morgan seemed to be getting pretty cozy there, Kayla wouldn't mind hanging out with her on the regular. Despite her small stature, she was badass without being cold.

Devon would really appreciate that too. Maybe they should go out some time.

"I appreciate you saying that and I'm sorry your family had their heads up their asses when it came to you."

"I'm just glad your brother and the rest of the Hot Rides gang have adopted me into their community." Sevan smiled softly then, making Kayla a tiny bit envious. "Give him a chance and he'll make sure you feel as welcome as I know you are." Sevan touched her forearm lightly. "I hadn't met Gavyn yet when he was really struggling, but I know the man he is now and I think you'll love this new version of him like we do."

"I guess that's why I'm here," Kayla admitted. "Or why I thought I was. I can come back."

"You're not leaving already, are you?" Amber drew their attention. She approached with her gorgeous baby boy balanced on her hip as she crossed the last of the lawn between them. "You just got here!"

"Hey." Kayla perked up at the sight of the little one.

Noah stared at her with eyes she would recognize anywhere.

Sevan's smile grew. "Your nephew is seriously the cutest damn kid. He's going to be a heart breaker just like the rest of the people around this place."

"Does that include you?" Amber teased, eying Sevan's shorts and the curve of her tight ass peeking out from beneath the frayed hem. "I think you're giving your guys a heart attack every time you bend over today."

"Gotta try to keep up." Sevan shrugged one shoulder and the corner of her mouth kicked up. Kayla thought she really was only now realizing how incredible she truly was.

When Amber leaned in for a hug, Noah smiled and cooed, but not at Kayla. At Sevan.

Of course, because he knew the mechanic and interacted with her every day, whereas Kayla was practically a stranger who'd only seen him a few times in person since he'd been born, although she tried to catch up with Gavyn and Amber on videochat periodically. She needed to make a real effort to do that more often.

Sevan greeted baby Noah and tickled him before Amber turned and tipped her torso toward Kayla. "Would you like to hold him?"

"If he wants me to." She held her hands out, and to her surprise, Noah reached for her. His miniature fists made grabby motions at her upper arms and she realized he was mesmerized by her colorful tattoos.

"Be careful he doesn't snatch one of your piercings." Amber put her hand on her face. "He doesn't have many manners yet."

"Or he's just not used to seeing women like me." Kayla wondered why all of a sudden she was so out of place.

Had losing Bare Natural been that big of a blow to her identity? Did it fundamentally change who she was or her self-worth? It had been a long damn time since she'd felt this insecure about who she was.

"What's that supposed to mean?" Amber asked cautiously. "You're obviously his coolest auntie."

Noah giggled as if he was agreeing with his mom, then latched onto one of the side braids Kayla had plaited her hair into that morning. She smiled down at him as he played with it, content to explore while the women talked.

"I guess I'm out of sorts." Kayla grimaced. "Probably not enough sleep and too much worry. Sorry."

Amber squished her then, and Noah rested the side of his face against his mother. It was a good damn thing Gavyn had figured out how to save his relationship with Amber before ruining it forever. She was a good person— a smart businesswoman, gorgeous, and perfect for Kayla's brother. She'd saved him even if she didn't realize it.

And for that, Kayla owed her an awful lot.

"Don't apologize. You have every right to be shook." Amber winced. "We saw the news. The devastation looks horrific. I'm sure it's even worse when it's your personal property and not some clip on TV."

Kayla nodded, surprised that tears prickled her eyes. What the hell was wrong with her? She wasn't the crying type and definitely never caved to emotion around people she didn't know near as well as her Powertools crew. Maybe it was hormones. Could she be going through menopause at thirty-eight?

Probably not.

She looked up at the sky and the fluffy clouds breezing past to clear the moisture away before it could leak out. Noah patted her cheek as if to tell her it would be okay.

"You know, Gavyn mentioned a plot of land for sale not too far from here and how awesome it would be for Bare Natural 2." Amber didn't meet Kayla's gaze when she dropped that bomb, but the weight of her suggestion hit Kayla square in the chest.

Especially after she'd seen what the area had to offer right down by the Hot Rods garage and the lake Joe's uncle Tom had graciously offered to sell him. It was idyllic, and filled with so much potential.

"He did?" If she hadn't been bouncing Noah, keeping him distracted so they could talk, she might have fallen flat on her ass.

"Yeah. You should talk to him about it." Amber cleared her throat. "I know he has his flaws, but he does have a head for business."

"Oh, come on," Sevan teased. "We know it's really you who's the mastermind behind Hot Rides."

"We do it together. But seriously, he's pretty smart about this stuff. Maybe he could help you think of ways not only to get back on your feet, but to turn this shitshow into a growth opportunity." Amber was gentle with her suggestion, and kind. It meant a lot that she'd encourage Kayla to be closer to their little family.

She nodded. "Will you let him know I stopped by and that I'd like to talk to him when he has some time for me?"

"He'll make time for you, Kayla," Amber promised. "If I called him right now and told him you need him, he'd break every speed limit to get here. I'm sorry if he hasn't always made you feel like that's the case."

"Oh." Kayla blinked, and this time there was no stopping the droplet that formed at the corner of her eye from spilling onto her cheek. She hated being this fragile.

"Don't do that. But yeah, I'll follow up with him sometime soon for sure. Thank you."

Noah shrieked and giggled as all three women surrounded him and cuddled him in the middle as they shared one last epic embrace. Then Amber and Noah joined her in raiding Devra and Morgan's bake session while Sevan returned to transforming that hunk of junk bike into a masterpiece.

Kayla felt lighter than she had in weeks. And wondered how long she could make the feeling last.

9
———

It had taken ten long, agonizing days—sped along only by the company she was keeping—but finally Kayla had gotten the call she'd been waiting for. A representative from her insurance company was going to meet her out at Bare Natural, or what little was left of it, the next morning.

They'd hurried back to Devon's place so Kayla could print out her paperwork, review everything, and try desperately to get a good night's rest before the big day.

Unfortunately, she was losing her mind instead. "Where the hell did I put the inventory list? I had it in my hand five minutes ago!"

She riffled through the previously neat and now disheveled papers on the cute desk in the corner of Neil, James, and Devon's living room. Her elbow caught the glass of water Dave had plunked down and ordered her to drink before he'd gone out to the yard to play some kind of sportsball with Neil and James. Of course, she knocked it over. Water spilled across her documentation before the pretty pale blue cup tumbled off the desk and smashed on the hardwood floor.

"Shit! Shit!" Kayla scooped up what remained of it with her bare hand as if that would put it back together.

She should know by now that some things couldn't be repaired.

"Kayla?" Devon popped her head in from the back porch where she'd been practicing some of the yoga moves Sabra and Holden had taught them while trying to help Kayla calm the fuck down in Middletown. It clearly wasn't working for her.

"I'm sorry. Shit. I broke it." She held her palm out, presenting the shards of glass.

"Be careful. You'll cut yourself. Here." Devon grabbed a trashcan and guided Kayla's hand so that she dumped the glittery bits into it.

Pissed that she didn't seem to be able to do anything right, not even get rid of the evidence of her mistakes, she snipped at Devon, "I'm not a child. I can clean this up."

Devon withdrew her fingers as if burned. "Okay then. Go ahead. But maybe you should watch where you're—"

"Ouch!" Kayla hopped on one foot as she plucked a sliver from the other. Fortunately it hadn't gone in deep."

"—stepping."

"What the hell is wrong with me?" Kayla sank to her knees and finished picking up the glass. She knelt there and stared up at Devon.

"Maybe you're forcing things too hard. Trying to make this happen when it's not meant to be." The other woman responded too fast to have thought of it in the moment. How long had she been waiting to say that?

"You think I should give up on Bare Natural?"

"I want you to see that things don't have to always

be like they were to be right." Devon said it calmly, but her honesty sliced Kayla's heart open as surely as if Devon had stabbed her with the broken glass. "But it's okay if you're not ready to hear that yet. Let's clean this up. I'll help you get ready for tomorrow and you can see what the insurance company has to say about it."

Devon might as well have smacked Kayla in the face. "What exactly is it you think they're going to tell me?"

"I'm on your side. I want you to get everything you're hoping for. I'm worried, though, about what will happen if you don't. Can you accept the verdict or not? What if they tell you it's a complete loss?" Devon asked softly.

"Then you'll get to celebrate. I'll give the fuck up and we can all move out to Middletown permanently. That's what you want, isn't it? To manage a crew of your own, like Mike and Joe?" Kayla blurted out her worst fears. "How long are you going to wait before you abandon us and do it anyway? Once the project is finished or before it even begins?"

"I'm not—"

"Well, you fucking should." Kayla didn't do as well as Devon at keeping calm, her talking becoming a shout. "What the hell are you doing hanging around here when you should be a foreman too? I don't want to be responsible for you not living up to your full potential. Not Dave or James or Neil either."

"Oh. I see. We've entered some sort of guilty bullshit phase." Devon stood up straighter. "I'm better at tough love than coddling. Work your feelings out with Dave and we can talk again when you're ready to put on your big girl panties. Fight for Bare Natural or don't. Keep it how it was or evolve. But don't you dare put this on me when I've always had your back and always will. Get your shit together, bitch."

Kayla jolted back. Devon had never lashed out at her like that in the years they'd known each other. Without a doubt, she'd deserved it. That didn't make it sting any less. Her face fell, but instead of fixing things, she only made them worse, flinging a reflexive suggestion like one of Morgan's chef knives. "Maybe it's best if Dave and I go. Find our own place."

And it hit its mark.

Devon recoiled. "You're not happy to have us around anymore? A few weeks turned out to be too much time together? It's like I don't even know you right now."

The last thing Kayla wanted was more fractures in the crew, but she didn't want to be the one causing them to stick somewhere they didn't belong. Right now she wished she could run away from it all, even the people she loved, because she felt like she was constantly letting them down. "Maybe you never did."

"You know what, maybe you're right." Devon crossed her arms. "Look, I'm your friend, but that doesn't mean I'm your punching bag. There's a difference between being supportive and being taken advantage of, and as much as I love you, I'm not going to let you cross that line."

"Fine. As soon as Dave gets back, we'll get out of your hair. Then you three can feel free to leave and return to your lives, uninterrupted." Kayla tossed up her hands. Just because it was the right thing didn't mean it made her skip and twirl to think of the last of their group leaving her and Dave behind. More like it eviscerated her. Maybe she was just scared it would happen when she least expected it. At least if she told them to go, she'd know it was coming. Her sanity couldn't withstand any more bombshells.

"You're hurting, you're disappointed, but lashing out at me isn't going to fix that." Devon held her arms out as if to hug Kayla, but she didn't deserve that kind of loyalty when she'd been such an ungrateful asshole and couldn't guarantee she wasn't going to be equally as miserable to be around for a while yet.

"You're right." Kayla turned her back on Devon. "I'm going to go pack. Please, leave me alone."

She jogged up the stairs to the bedroom she'd been sharing with Dave, Devon, James, and Neil but her friend didn't follow.

Instead, Devon did exactly as she'd been asked.

Kayla's heart shattered.

10

———

"**K**ayla? What's going on?" Dave peeked through the bedroom door as if he expected to have to duck or maybe tuck and roll.

Ugh. It wasn't like she was going to launch her suitcase at his face or something.

She didn't need her husband or their friends to be afraid of her. That wasn't the kind of person she was. Except maybe she was becoming volatile, running hot and cold like the water that would singe then freeze you in a shitty hotel, and that only made her more upset.

When she didn't respond right away, he clarified, "Devon just ran through the kitchen looking like she was about to cry."

"Ah, fuck." Kayla buried her face in her hands. The last thing she wanted was to hurt the people who always had her back, but she felt like she was doing that no matter what she tried. "Go after her. Tell her I'm stupid and I'm sorry."

"No." He crossed his arms and spread his feet. He

wasn't often so serious, and she found it kind of turned her on. Damn, she really was completely out of control.

"No?" She tested him.

"I will not do that. James and Neil will make sure she's okay, and if I hear you say such bullshit about yourself again I'm going to get pissed. Enough." Dave strode to her and drew himself up to his full height, which he rarely did. His stormy gray eyes were way, way up there as he peered down at her. "Tell me what's going on."

"I don't know. I feel...confused." Kayla went slack, her arms hanging at her sides. "Nothing is the same. Everything I thought I knew about myself is gone and keeps changing."

"Everything?" Dave asked, rubbing her shoulders.

"Okay, no. I'm so glad I have you." She hugged him so tight he let out an *oof*. "Without you and the crew I would really be drifting right now. What seems right one minute feels completely wrong the next. It's scary and freaking me out. So don't you do that to me, too. Don't let go no matter what, okay?"

"Never." Dave crushed her to him, helping her relax. He sighed. "Life isn't a straight path, Kayla. We've been lucky it's been a while since the road we were on took a sharp turn, but as long as we're traveling it together, everything's going to be okay."

She took a deep breath and then another as what he said sank in. "You're right."

"I know, because I learned that from you." He pulled her back far enough that he could stare into her eyes. "After my accident you saved me. So let me be there for you now. Not that I think you need rescuing, but I want to at least hold your hand while you kick ass and start off in whatever new direction you decide to go in."

Kayla blinked up at her husband, wondering how she got so damn lucky in life. She'd do well to remember exactly how much she had to be grateful for, starting with him. "You're sexy as hell, you know that?"

Dave laughed, turning a bit pink under his silvery scruff. "That wasn't the reaction I thought I'd get but, hey, I'll take it."

"What else will you take?" Kayla turned seductive, needing for one moment to have some control. And here, with her husband, she knew exactly how to put herself in charge, even when he took the lead.

"Are you telling me you want to make love with me?" Dave asked, tipping his head. "Now? In the middle of all this? You've already had a rough day. Are you sure?"

"Don't bruise my ego. It's already taken a big enough hit lately." Kayla hesitated. "I need you."

"I'm not saying no, believe me." Dave advanced until his hands rested on her hips. They were so big, they constantly impressed her, reminding her of how strong he was and how safe he would keep her. "Do I ever say no to you?"

"You did a minute ago. And I kind of liked it." She grinned until he growled and covered her hint of a smile with his lips.

Dave wasn't gentle like James or smooth like Joe. He was blunt and direct and a little bit unwieldy at times. She loved that about him. How he was raw and real and, most of all, hers. She loved that about him best.

She put her arms around his neck and hopped, wrapping her legs around his muscled waist. He clutched her, grabbing her butt, but still, he staggered a bit off balance with his bum leg.

She didn't doubt he could handle it, though. Handle

her. So she clung to him and busied herself with nuzzling his neck, breathing deep of the scent of spice and soap that she associated with him and comfort. She kissed his jaw as he walked her backward and crashed to Devon, Neil, and James's bed face up.

"Is it weird to get it on in our friends' bed without them in it?" Dave wondered as they bounced.

"Serves Devon right." Kayla knew she was being petty and that her argument with the other woman had been mostly her fault. But she couldn't think about that right then or she'd lose her mojo.

"We can make it up to them later." Dave kissed Kayla softly, taking away the lingering ache from her argument. Figures he'd understand she needed that.

He rubbed her back as he nudged the straps of her tank top off her shoulders. And in between one breath and the next he'd gotten rid of it. How he managed to do it with his thick fingers, she wouldn't ever figure out, but he was adept at unhooking her bra and helping her shed the rest of her clothes.

And then she was doing her part to get rid of his, pushing his shirt up until she couldn't reach any higher and he took over, ripping it above his head and dropping it to the ground, utterly forgotten.

Kayla couldn't wait to feel his skin against hers, to know that he was there and this at least would never change. She grinned as he huffed out an annoyed sound and grasped her hips, aligning her on top of him so that the proof of his arousal was unmistakable between her legs. She sat up a bit, eager to be joined with him, but he stopped her from undulating over his cock.

She tipped her head and glanced at him from beneath

heavy lids. He was like the world's best pain reliever, numbing her until she could recover.

"Not so fast," he said, his voice sounding like he'd breathed in too much of the smoke that still lingered in the air around town.

"Faster," she argued, and reached for his thick erection.

"Nope." Dave shook his head, then lifted her, proving that although his leg might not be as strong as he liked, other parts of him more than made up for it. Muscles flexed in the thick columns of his arms. She squirmed in his hold. He didn't budge.

Dave raised her over his abs and then his chest until he settled her core over his face and her legs folded on either side of his head.

"Oh." She quit fighting when he craned his neck upward so that he could lick along her entire slit, his nose prodding her clit. Instead she leaned back, bracing herself on his pecs, relishing his heart pounding beneath her palm. He wasn't only doing this for her. He loved it as much as she did.

Kayla arched her back, presenting herself to him. He accepted her invitation and feasted on her flesh. His tongue snaked up into her, spearing her with a slick warmth that made her fingers curl in his light chest hair. He didn't seem to mind the slight indentation of her nails there and instead redoubled his efforts.

The problem with Dave going down on her was that he was too damn good at it. It never lasted very long because he knew her so fucking well. He got off on making her come, hard, and took it as a personal challenge to give her as much pleasure as possible.

She was not complaining.

Kayla shivered when he raked his teeth over the metal rings in her labia. Those piercings were one of the best things she'd ever decided to try. They enhanced every motion of his lips, tongue, and teeth, nuzzling her with just the right tension to add another level to his touches. And when he began to suck on her clit, gently tugging the bar through her hood, her thighs quivered around his cheeks.

His rumble of laughter, like distant thunder providing an early warning of an approaching summer storm, did nothing to keep her from climbing higher. Dave lifted his hands and filled them with her breasts. His thumbs arced over the lower swell and to her nipples like windshield wipers. Except instead of swiping away rain, he was toying with the piercings there too.

He knew all of her weak spots. And only used them to her benefit.

Kayla tried not to suffocate him as her muscles tensed, and instead began to rock over his mouth, trying to urge him to continue. He didn't need much goading.

Dave concentrated on her clit, pulsing his suction. She assumed he was trying to present her with an appetizer in what would surely become an afternoon buffet of pleasures. So she didn't fight it.

She closed her eyes and let herself enjoy the rapture he was treating her to.

And though she wanted more, yearned to be full of him, joined with him, staring into his eyes as they experienced this together, she let herself be selfish first. Kayla drew in a deep shaky breath and let it out on a moan. Dave sucked on her harder, adding a swirl of his tongue that was sure to set her off.

Kayla froze, then launched into a flurry of motion as her muscles clenched, held, and released in a quick climax that left her tingling all over and eager for more. She shifted, crawling backward until her legs straddled Dave's hips again and she could drape herself over his wide torso. She laid her head on his shoulder and tried to catch her breath even as her entire body was singing with bliss.

Before she could, he tipped her face up and kissed her, staring into her eyes to observe her dilated pupils and the ecstasy he'd brought her washing over her features. She was happy to be wrecked for him, showing him with the glides of her lips over his just how appreciative she was of him and his intimate knowledge of what she required most—in bed and out.

He smothered her, sheltering her from the rest of the world as he took her pleasure and amplified it. She writhed on him, the length of his cock rubbing against her mound and the lower part of her stomach.

She pushed up on straight-locked arms and pouted a bit for effect. "You're not going to hold out on me again, are you?"

He rubbed his nose over hers and chuckled. "I'm not a saint."

"I much prefer bad boys." She nibbled his lower lip, then levered herself upright so she was kneeling over him again, except this time she planned to be the one doing some of the tempting and teasing. She highly doubted he'd let her win and come with her this next time, though. That wasn't his style. He liked to drag things out, fully exhaust her, today probably more than most.

She needed this. Needed the release, the diversion from reality, and the stress reduction that came from a half dozen or so good orgasms. She probably needed to talk to the insurance rep about taking out a special policy on Dave's dick in case she broke it with all the medicinal sex she was going to prescribe herself to make it through the next year or so.

"Put me inside you," he told her.

Kayla lifted up enough to angle his cock toward between her legs. Of course she took the opportunity to stroke him a few, okay maybe a dozen, times.

When his eyes grew heavy, she pounced, sliding him along the length of her so she could get him nice and slippery. Even now, he was sometimes a little much, especially in this position. Kayla couldn't wait for sensation to consume her and positive feelings to override the sickness she'd felt when she saw Devon's face twisted in anguish.

Dave gripped her waist and shook her a bit. "Focus on me. This. We can work out the rest later."

Kayla swallowed hard and directed his cock toward her core. She sank over it, the blunt tip wedging inside her until she allowed gravity to help her slide downward. His hands were there, slowing her descent, always careful not to let her rush and risk causing herself even the slightest bit of pain.

"I've got you," he promised. "I'm here, remember?"

Kayla bit her lip and nodded. She should have gone to find him when her emotions started to bubble over but she'd been scared and dumb and...

"Later." He held her still and rocked up a bit more, feeding her another inch or two of his shaft.

She concentrated on what he was doing to her body, lighting it up and making it sing. It only took a few more seconds of them working together to fuse their bodies for her intruding thoughts to evaporate. And when she held him fully within her, she breathed out a sigh of relief.

"That's better. When you're ready, ride me." He petted her flank then reached around to smack her ass. She might have been on top, but he owned her heart and soul.

Kayla did as he instructed. She found their perfect pace, his cock rubbing the most sensitive places within her, nudging the spot that made her see stars even if they weren't in their woods on a warm summer night. He cupped her shoulder, then guided her lower, so their chests brushed across each other, and toyed with her piercings.

But when he kissed her, soft and slow and filled with compassion, she broke.

Kayla worked over him as he thrust upward, making sure they came fully together on each stroke and that his pelvis massaged her clit. It wasn't long before her thighs were trembling, and not from the strain of holding herself above him.

"Yeah. Come on me. Let me feel you fly." He massaged her back and bit her neck in the spot right below her ear that was guaranteed to set her off.

Kayla shouted his name and clenched the sheets in her fists as she shuddered, climaxing for the second time that afternoon. She didn't have a moment to catch her breath before Dave was rolling over, taking her to her back and continuing to grind into her, refusing to let her settle completely before lifting her up again.

If he wobbled a bit on his bad leg, she didn't even bother to offer to change positions. He was fully capable of fucking her, and if he had to take a break he'd say so. In that moment, she realized that she should be more like him and ask for support when she needed it.

If she'd told him before that her anxiety was building again, maybe they could have done this first and she wouldn't have taken out her frustrations on Devon.

"You're still not with me one-hundred percent," he paused. "Do you want me to stop?"

It wasn't a threat—he was genuinely asking. And the fact that he'd walk away now when he so obviously was nearing his own satisfaction after giving her seconds only made her love him that much more.

"Don't you dare." She set her nails into his back just enough to show him she was serious.

In response, he began to fuck in earnest, their bodies slapping together in time to their groans. She was surprised when she felt herself about to peak again, or maybe she was still high on the last orgasm. This time she couldn't even give him so much as a warning.

Her body tipped, clenching around him, hugging him tight as she came and came.

A bead of sweat rolled down his temple but he still resisted joining her, making her a little worried they wouldn't share the sweetness of a simultaneous release together that afternoon. But she wasn't about to tell him to stop before he'd experienced the same rapture he'd given her. It would only make her feel like she'd let him down again.

"I swear," he grunted, then pulled out, making her gasp his name. But she should have realized he wasn't done with her yet. He flipped her over, placed his forearm across her shoulders, then leaned in on her, pinning her down as he held himself up.

Her mind blanked out, finally free of anything but the

weight of him over her and the mass of him filling her when he plunged back inside. He sagged a bit, resting completely on her, heavier on one side as he gave his tortured thigh a break.

He held her close to him as he kept working behind her, getting impossibly deep in this position. His hand slid beneath her and his fingers targeted her clit, pinching it a bit as he hammered into her, making the bed protest.

That was the only thing complaining.

Kayla screamed his name and let go, giving herself over to him. She was pretty sure she had nothing left in reserve when he leaned down and bit her shoulder right before his strokes turned jerky. He roared and thrust into her fully one last time before yielding to his own orgasm. As he seared her with his release, she came too, the relief so intense she nearly passed out.

Kayla wasn't sure if she had fallen into a nap or if she was so relaxed that she zoned out for a while, with Dave sheltering her in his arms, until footsteps climbing the stairs had him tensing and rousing her too. She went to her elbow on the bed and drew the sheet over her and Dave.

But she shouldn't have bothered. Because it was James who stuck his head into the bedroom and looked around, grinning when he saw them tangled up in his sheets.

"I found them!" he called over his shoulder. "And I think they were having fun without us."

Kayla lifted her head from Dave's chest long enough to wink at him.

"Hey! The rules are no one gets to come in my bed unless I do too." Neil bounded up the stairs next. Devon tailed him, looking unsure, something that didn't suit her at all.

"Well, you better catch up then." Dave scooted over, still clutching Kayla to his warm, solid body. "Don't mind if we watch because I'm not moving any time soon."

"If you play spectator you might be ready for round two sooner than you think." James raised a brow, as if he wouldn't mind that one bit.

Kayla might have believed she was exhausted and utterly satisfied only moments ago but the idea had her tingling all over. Especially because she felt an epic need to repair the rift she'd hewn in her relationship with Devon earlier. "Why don't you take that as a challenge then? Let me see you spoil your lovely wife. And we'll see where things take us."

Hopefully Devon would accept that as the olive branch Kayla intended it to be.

"I hope you know I'll always do my best for you," Devon said, quieter and more seriously.

"I do, even if I'm a shit friend and can't always claim the same. I'm sorry for what I said before and how I acted. Truly." Kayla reached out and squeezed Devon's fingers.

"Things are rough right now. I know you didn't mean it." Devon squeezed back.

"Damn it," Neil groused. "I was hoping there would be lady wrestling or maybe makeup sex."

"Shut up, start taking care of your wife, and maybe there will be yet." Dave adjusted himself on a stack of pillows, propping up both himself and Kayla so they had a perfect view of the trio, who began stripping on their bed.

It was hours later that they fell into a pile together—exhausted, happy, and definitely anything but angry at each other.

Something in Kayla's life was exactly how it had

always been meant to be. Hopefully tomorrow would put more things back in order.

She closed her eyes and fell asleep surrounded by people who loved her and always would, even on her worst days.

11

Kayla's heart beat as hard as the bass at the rock festival she'd taken Dave to last summer. They'd been summoned back from Middletown after ten days so that she could meet with the insurance appraiser. Except when she pulled up, alone—because she'd somehow felt like dealing with this head-on and solo would prove to herself that she wasn't losing her ability to adult somehow—she was shocked to see three other vehicles and a few men with clipboards and bright orange vests roaming the site where her home and business used to stand.

She climbed from her car and shut the door a little too hard, the slam echoing through the still mountain air now that there wasn't a riot of trees and other foliage to deaden the sound.

The men turned toward her and approached, none of them looking especially chipper.

"Good morning," she said with a nod.

"It is morning," one responded before sticking out his

hand. "I'm not sure this is anyone's definition of good, though. I'm sorry."

Kayla nodded and stared into his eyes as they shook. Then she did the same with the other two guys. It was better than looking over at the ruins of her hard work and the love she'd poured into this place.

"I'm Lance. I'm the claims specialist. This is Bruce, our engineer, and that's Carl, our environmental impact guru." He gestured to each one in turn.

"Wow. I didn't realize we'd need all that today." Kayla toyed with the piercing in her lip. "It seems pretty obvious to me that this is a shut and dry case. There's nothing left. I brought our construction records, receipts, and inventories to verify the value covered by the policy." She held out the four-inch binder of documentation she'd compiled.

"Well, at least you're accepting of that." Lance sighed as if he'd been afraid to say what they all could obviously see. "We can appraise the land value and cut you a check, but there's not going to be anything up here for a very long time. It sure must have been pretty before."

"Wait, what?" Kayla stammered.

Bruce winced. "You weren't planning on rebuilding on site, were you?"

"Yes. This is my home. The place I've invested the last nearly twenty years of my life. I'm not going anywhere."

"Ah, shit." He looked to Lance. Guess he didn't get paid enough to deal with the raving madwoman he assumed she was about to become.

"Ma'am—"

"Don't. My name is Kayla."

"Kayla." Lance turned and motioned for her to follow.

"Let me show you something and Carl can explain what we're looking at here."

He led them over to the brink of a steep drop-off, where her house had perched to optimize its view out onto the lake. The rest of the land sloped a little more gradually beyond where the cabins had been, but from here she noticed slashes in the mountainside that she hadn't seen before, focused on her home and the property itself.

"What's that?" She eyed the ragged lines that stair-stepped down the mountain.

Carl pointed to some of the other evidence of heavy machinery she'd assumed were from the firetrucks and other emergency workers. "When they fight the fire, they often cut into the terrain to prevent mudslides and other erosion effects. This is unstable land. Dangerous. It will take years and lots of reforestation, mature trees, and established groundcover before the mountain you knew is ready for people to resettle it and safe enough for you to erect the kinds of structures you had here before."

"*Years*?" Kayla nearly choked. "We don't have years. We need to start construction in the spring, latest. Is there any way that's possible? My husband is part owner of a construction company. We have access to a lot of resources other people might not."

"I mean...possible? Sure. But..." Bruce looked over to Carl, who shook his head no.

"Don't tell me why it can't be done, tell me how it can be and let me decide if it's worth it." Kayla refused to quit now.

"You'd need to regrade the entire hill. They'd have to put in supports first. Either wooden railroad ties or some kind of steel mesh. Then terrace the mountainside from your entrance all the way down to the lake. No more natural slope. On top of that you'd have to landscape it to lock in the soil. You'd need a dedicated crew of about twenty people, working full time, the entire winter, and a miracle number of good-weather days to get it done in six months. Once the ground is frozen..."

"You're telling me about problems again, not solutions." Kayla pinched the bridge of her nose as she realized the scale of the hurdle she was facing. This one might be the one she couldn't clear, no matter how hard she tried. "Ballpark, how much would that cost, if it was possible?"

"Three million? Maybe more?" Bruce sighed. "I'm sorry to ruin your day, but put it this way: my company wouldn't even put in a bid on a job like that. It's just not going to happen."

"I can confirm that." Lance frowned. "Unless you've got some other source of disposable income, the payout we're going to write for your policy isn't going to be a drop in the bucket of what you'll need."

"Fuck!" Kayla hissed.

"I'm sorry. Really." Lance tried his best to soften the blow. "There are plenty of beautiful spots in the next county over. My wife is a real estate agent. I could give you her number."

"No, thank you," Kayla snapped without thinking. It was a reflex to deny that she was going to do anything but soldier on. Although, she should probably start considering it.

Maybe it was time to admit defeat.

"Okay. Well, here's my card if you change your mind or have any follow up questions later. I hope things work out like you want." Lance held the paper on his clipboard out to her. It said pretty much exactly what he'd already told her. They were going to write off Bare Natural, the land, and everything that had been inside it and her home. They'd pay out her claim, but there was no way it'd be enough to rebuild there. And even if she did, they wouldn't cover her at that location ever again. "You can take it to a lawyer to review if you want, but we'll need it signed before we can write you a check."

Kayla took the copy he offered her and tucked it into the front pocket of her useless binder. "At a minimum I want to talk it over with my husband and the rest of the people in his crew before making a decision."

"I understand. It's a lot to process." Why the hell did Lance have to be kind? It would have been easier to be pissed at him if he and his band of merry experts had been assholes.

"Thank you. I...have to go." Numbness tingled along her limbs until she couldn't feel her fingers or toes or the tip of her tongue. Kayla turned away. Seeing Bare Natural burn had been bad, but this...this was the end. She was done. It was over.

For good.

All she wanted was to go home, crawl in her bed, and bawl. But she'd lost that too. And now she doubted she'd ever come back to this spot again. It hurt too fucking much.

Dave, Devon, James, and Neil were the closest thing she had to a safe haven here. She hoped they were ready to put up with her hysteria because she wasn't sure how she was even going to hold it together until she pulled into their driveway.

12

Since there hadn't been anything to keep them at home, Kayla had suggested that they go on one more trip to Middletown while she tried to work up the courage to scribble her name on that piece of paper that felt like a death sentence. No one had argued. At least in Middletown Dave, Devon, Neil, and James could help Mike and Joe instead of sitting around with their thumbs up their asses while absolutely nothing got done at Bare Natural and Kayla sank further into depression and self-doubt.

But once they'd arrived, there was really only one person she felt like talking to: Gavyn.

Since her last visit, and her discussion with Amber and Sevan, he'd been texting her periodically. Reaching out even if she hadn't reciprocated as much as she should have, caught up in everything going on. It felt nice to know he cared and that he was checking up on her, though she was afraid she hadn't shown him how much it meant while she was trapped in the slog of trying to make something impossible happen.

Kayla walked from Morgan and Joe's rental to Hot Rides. It was a bit of a hike, but the trek through the late summer woods, with dappled light spilling through the leaves and the chirping of birds reminding her so much of the place she'd loved more than any other, had done a lot to settle her nerves.

Because she'd been kicking around a few different options for where to go next, and she wondered what Gavyn might think. What if he didn't believe any of them was a good idea?

She stumbled over a stick in the path, barely catching herself before she face-planted.

Sometimes disasters weren't so easy to avert, though.

If she committed to a vision for the future, she wasn't the kind of person to let anything stand in her way. Laws of nature aside. Fuck erosion. So if he wasn't onboard with a change of direction, one that meant she'd be spending a lot more time in his backyard, it could make things awkward between her and her brother. As much as she hated to admit it, she wasn't ready to jeopardize her last strong tie to her family.

Kayla turned into the Hot Rides driveway, feeling the burn in her muscles. She kept her pace while climbing the fairly steep slope. Instead of going to the shop, she peeled off early, and headed for Gavyn and Amber's house.

They weren't so different, after all, her and her brother. They both had businesses and lived on site. They gave everything they had to the enterprises, making them part of their daily existence. Was that fair to the people they loved most? Their spouses?

Neither Dave nor Amber had ever seemed to mind, supporting their visions in any way possible. Hell, Amber was an amazing project manager, and she for sure had been the one to rein Gavyn in and make his wild imaginings into something that wasn't only reality, but something profitable too.

The garage was always full. Even now the sound of power tools and laughter spilled from the open garage bays where Trevon, Quinn, Wren, Ollie, Walker, Dane, and Sevan were busy with any number of special projects.

Kayla probably should have gone there first, talked to Gavyn in his office without pulling him away from his work, but she was reaching out for advice as his sister and not as a fellow business owner. She also hoped to signal her desire to have his full attention for once, whether it was selfish to admit that or not.

The question was, would he have time for her at all? She was about to put Amber's theory to the test.

Kayla raised her hand to knock on the door, but before she could, Amber was there, opening it wide and welcoming her inside. At least she'd gotten lucky there. Amber was an incredible sister-in-law and never once had made her feel like a burden. She hoped Amber and Gavyn felt the same about Dave, who would give his good leg for anyone he knew, never mind family.

"Hey, I heard you were back in town." Amber hugged Kayla, making her blink for a moment. "I'm sorry you didn't get the news you wanted about the site."

Kayla should have figured news traveled fast among their tight-knit community.

"I appreciate that." She sighed, lacking the energy to pretend like it hadn't been a devastating blow. "I guess it's time to start thinking out of the box and face the fact that I can't go back. Things will never be like they were."

"It's hard to let go." Amber nodded. "Good things are

waiting for you. And if there's anything we can do to help, Gavyn and I are here for you."

"About that...I'm hoping I can talk to him today." Kayla tried to keep her tone even and casual, but it sounded squeaky and tense, even to her.

"Let me go over to the shop and let him know you're here." Amber smiled softly. "He'll be with you in just a second, I promise. Crash on the couch or something. Make yourself at home."

"Thanks." Kayla wandered into the sunny living room with a high, peaked ceiling. She trailed her fingertips over the surface of a dark wood table that held framed pictures —Gavyn breaking ground at Hot Rides, a portrait of him and Amber, several candid snaps of baby Noah. Her heart hitched when she saw one of Gavyn with his arm slung around her at her wedding.

It was a day he didn't remember, and she sometimes wished she couldn't.

Not because of the ceremony part, but for what had come after, when he'd fallen ever so spectacularly off the wagon. It made her angry and sad all over again because the best day of her life had also been one of the worst. She had to keep a lot of parts of that day, like her copy of this same photograph, locked away in a dark drawer where she didn't take them out to examine them for fear of hurting Gavyn or reminding him of how close he'd come to losing everything, including his life.

Then again, this might be the only wedding photo she had left. Her guts cramped and she made a mental note to ask the rest of the crew for any they'd taken.

As she was staring at the image, lost in thought, Gavyn cleared his throat from behind her. "It was an amazing day. I'm still so sorry I fucked it up for you."

"You didn't ruin anything for me. You screwed it up for yourself." She sighed and turned, not wanting him to misunderstand.

"So badly." He grimaced.

And like always, she had the urge to change the topic because she wasn't trying to make him feel worse than he already did or, god forbid, propel him into a downward spiral that resulted in him relapsing. It had already eaten at her so bad that he'd binged on the alcohol they'd served at the wedding. She never should have allowed it, even if their other alcoholic friend—Roman—had given it the green light.

Gavyn and Roman had gone through rehab together. To this day, she thought ignoring that fact and not accommodating for their disease was one of the most irresponsible and inconsiderate things she'd ever done. She deserved for her relationship with Gavyn to be strained after putting him in that situation.

"So what's up, little sister?" He nudged her playfully with his elbow before swiping a baby toy from the loveseat and sinking into the plush cushion.

Kayla shrugged, finding it hard to form the words now that she was there, with him.

"I heard you got some more shit news about Bare Natural. I'm sorry."

She nodded. "It sucks. I think I'm at the point where I have to admit to myself that this isn't going to work before I waste more of everyone's time on a stupid delusion."

"Hey, don't talk like that." Gavyn sat forward, putting his elbows on his knees. "First of all, Dave and the rest of the crew would do anything for you. They'll keep working on this as long as you need them."

"I know, and that's why it's my responsibility to make

sound decisions." It hurt to say it out loud. Literally stole the air out of her lungs and made her deflate. She bent over, putting her hands on her knees.

"Sit down," Gavyn told her.

"I can't." It was bad enough she had to wear clothes, which irritated the hell out of her after years of roaming freely around her naturist resort, but now she was also cooped up inside, unable to escape the pressures of everything building around her.

"Okay, fine." He held his palms out. Then said, "But no matter what, trying to keep your resort alive is not dumb. It wasn't a bad idea when you first built it and it's definitely not now that you have an established brand even if you need to restructure it. Maybe you have to accept that it won't look exactly like it did before."

"Yeah, so...about that..." She tried to take a deep breath but couldn't past the bands restricting her chest. "It seems like Mike and Joe are going in a new direction, making something bigger of Powertools with the Hot Rods expansion project and now this new deal that's in the works with Giovanni for a mega tattoo shop that anchors some weekend getaway destination. Their hearts are here. Every time they talk about expanding Powertools and each of them managing their own crews, they get like some massive hard-on."

"Hey, I don't need to know about what you do in bed together." Gavyn covered his eyes with his hand. "It's bad enough I hear about the Hot Rods' adventures from Nola."

Kayla laughed, thinking of Amber's sister, who was part of the poly group over at the Hot Rods restoration garage. Nola loved to antagonize Amber and share the juicy details of their sessions, even some made-up ones for extra effect. "I meant metaphorically, but... well..."

Gavyn groaned. And with the mood lightened she blurted out the thought that had been weighing heavy on her heart. "I think I could be really successful if I moved the resort here and tweaked the concept. What do you think about that?"

"Really?" Gavyn's eyes went wide and Kayla forgot to breathe for long enough that the room began to spin. He asked again, "Are you serious?"

There was no taking it back now.

Kayla nodded. "I mean, if it wouldn't intrude on you too much."

"*Intrude*? What the fuck?" Gavyn cocked his head. "I would love to have you here. Close by. I mean, unless you don't want people knowing I'm your brother or getting up in your shit all the time. I would give you space if you need it."

"Huh?" Kayla felt her heart flip-flop. "Don't you know how proud I am of you? Of all you've done and how you've built Hot Rides from the ground up?"

And how you've straightened your life out. She didn't have the guts to say that part, though.

"Then why would you think twice about moving to Middletown?" Gavyn had gone pale. Maybe those old ghosts still haunted him as much as they did her. They should have hashed this out a long time ago.

"I didn't know if I'd really be welcome or if I'm another branch of our rotten family tree that you're trying your best to escape." Kayla tugged on her lip piercing with her teeth.

"Damn it, Kayla. I know we drifted apart, and that when we started to get tight again, I fucked it all up. But we still could be tight. Especially now that I have my shit together and I'm sober. And that goes twice as much for if you were here in Middletown. It would be great for Noah to have his favorite aunt in his life, in person instead of on a screen or only at holidays."

Sure, that stuff was a huge bonus. But could it be everything? If he didn't think the resort would flourish here, then could she junk the whole concept and start completely over in a new direction? Maybe go back to being a masseuse at someone else's establishment. Kayla didn't think her heart was in that.

"Is it copping out to quit now? To give up on Bare Natural and walk away from everything I've worked so damn hard for?" Kayla swung around. She hadn't realized she still harbored resentment from the days Gavyn had let her, and himself mostly, down over and over until it bubbled to the surface. "Some of us stick to our commitments and take pride in keeping our word. In taking care of what's ours."

Gavyn's face fell. He jerked, his shoulders crashing into the back of Amber's pretty furniture.

"I'm sorry." Kayla covered her mouth. "I didn't mean that."

"Yeah, you did. That's okay. It's me who's sorry, little sis." Gavyn scrubbed his hand over his face. "I let you down. You, Mom, Dad, the rest of our family. Repeatedly. And I can't ever change that."

Kayla followed her instincts. She crossed to him and climbed into his lap, hugging him tight like she had the time she was five or six and a tornado had skirted their family's country estate. Of course their parents had been working late—at some board meeting or fundraiser, as usual—but Gavyn had been there. And sure, maybe he'd been absent for a while too, but he'd found his way back to them.

"Sometimes the past is better left behind us." Gavyn rubbed her back like he had that scary night and she imagined how good of a father he was going to be to Noah. So much better than their own. "Even if you could put everything in place exactly as it had been right now, would you ever really be able to get the memory of the smoke smell or all that blackness from your mind? Or would you see it everywhere you looked? Would you be afraid that it could happen again?"

He looked down at her and she could tell he was thinking of his own personal disaster that had occurred at Bare Natural during the Powertools wedding. The night he'd almost killed himself, ruined his relationship with his would-be wife, but instead turned it all around.

He'd never set foot on the property again, and he was right. Neither would she.

"I guess sometimes you have to lose everything before you can start over," she whispered.

His eyes filled with tears, freaking her the fuck out. Gavyn *never* cried.

"Yeah, you're exactly right." He looked up at the ceiling until the glassiness subsided. "Though you might not think so in this moment, I swear to you, it's possible to claw your way back and be happier than you've ever been in your entire life. Even after you've burned everything to the ground."

Well, shit. He would know about that.

If Gavyn could do it, so could she....with a hell of a lot of help from the crew, and him.

"You'd really be happy if I moved to Middletown?" Kayla cleared her throat, unwilling to cave to the emotions clawing at her if Gavyn wasn't going to either. He was right. Together they were stronger.

"Ecstatic." He squeezed her tight. "Maybe I could start to restore some of the things I wrecked myself. Our relationship. Your trust in me. Stuff that matters way more than possessions, although I know they were precious to you."

Kayla leaned her head on his shoulder. It had only been the year before that they'd unexpectedly lost one of their brothers to a stroke. There one day. Gone the next. Dropped dead at his shiny executive desk. And for what? "I would like that too. Before it's too late."

"It's *never* too late," Gavyn promised her. "Stay here and I'll help you, Kayla. I swear. I'll be there every day doing whatever I can to make your wildest dreams come true. Even brighter than before. I mean, as long as you wear some damn clothes while I'm around."

She laughed at that. "You know, I was thinking..."

"Yeah?" He pulled back and tipped his head to the side, really listening to what she was saying as if her ideas mattered and her thoughts were valuable.

"What if I kept only a small part of the resort for naturists, but expanded the overall footprint and offerings? I think a full spa up front would go over well with the travel getaway concept Mike and Giovanni are collaborating on. And why pigeonhole myself? I was running some numbers before this happened about the profitability of weekenders and hosting special events. Devra and Morgan might be interested in catering them, which would be even better. I didn't pursue those kinds of bookings before because Bare Natural already had a reputation that was going to make it difficult for some people to take us seriously or feel comfortable hosting a wedding or other formal occasions there..."

"A wider audience?" Gavyn hummed. "Not a bad approach. Niche is good. You were always booked solid, but land is way cheaper out here. You could easily have five times as many cabins if you wanted and room to spread out and isolate your more risqué clientele."

For the first time since she'd stood before the wreckage of her home and choked on the fumes rising off the ashes of Bare Natural, Kayla got excited.

"Yeah. I could." She did some quick calculations. "With the settlement the insurance company is willing to offer me right now to write the place off... I absolutely could afford enough land to have different areas with enough separation that no one would have to worry about a bare booty photobombing their parents' fiftieth anniversary party portraits. I think I need to talk to Tom about that stretch down by the lake."

"It would be perfect, Kayla." Gavyn hugged her, then put his hands on her shoulders. "You can do this. I believe in you. I always have, and I won't let my own demons keep me from showing you how much ever again."

Kayla suddenly realized she had gotten lucky. Instead of being angry at the world, she was grateful. It may have given her exactly what she needed even though she hadn't realized it at the time.

"You know what? You're right, Gavyn." Kayla climbed from his arms, missing their strength but looking forward to telling Dave what she'd decided because she knew he'd be there to embrace her in his own, very non-fraternal way, along with her new aspirations. "Sometimes dreams die and new ones take their place. This is my future and I can't wait for you to share it with me."

"Thank you for giving me another chance." Gavyn stood and crushed her in a hug that she returned with interest.

"I'm glad the universe gave us both this opportunity." She stepped back and asked, "Do you have a pen?"

He blinked, then took one from the drawer of the side table. Kayla whipped out the paper that had been crumpled in her back pocket, signed it, and said, "I have to go send this to the insurance company and get this project rolling."

"Tell me what you need. Anything, Kayla, and I'll do it," Gavyn promised her.

"I just need you to love me." Her voice distorted as she told him the truth.

"I do. So very much."

"I love you too, big brother." Before they both could break down, she stood on her tiptoes to kiss his cheek, then headed for the door. "Tell your wife and son I love them too. And that Dave and I will be coming over for dinner sometime very soon."

"I will, and I can't wait." Gavyn was smiling wider than she'd seen in a while when she looked over her shoulder, waved, then started making her new dream a reality.

13

D ave walked beside Kayla as they climbed the stairs to Uncle Tom and Ms. Brown's house beside the Hot Rods garage. He would stand by her side whenever she asked, and even if she didn't. "You're going to do fine. This is practically family, okay?"

"That makes it harder." She squeezed his fingers where they were intertwined. "I don't want them to say yes out of pity or some shit, you know?"

"They respect you too much to be anything but fair," Dave reassured her as they knocked on the door.

Joe was already inside with his cousin Eli and Eli's dad, Tom. It was crowded around the dining room table but Ms. Brown; Eli's husband and wife, Sally and Alanso; and Joe's wife, Morgan, were all waiting for them.

Ms. Brown and Tom greeted them with wide smiles and wider arms. Dave and Kayla took the empty seats on the other side of Joe then made small talk while Tom offered them some of the goodies Ms. Brown had baked earlier that day.

Dave knew better than to turn down one of her

amazing chocolate-chip cookies. He'd already stuffed an entire one into his mouth when Tom asked Kayla, "So what is it you wanted to talk about?"

She peered over at Dave, who smiled encouragingly, or at least he hoped that was the vibe she got despite his lips being covered in gooey chocolate and crumbs. A soft laugh and a shake of her head broke her tension before she faced Tom directly and said, "I want to buy the land by the lake and develop it as the site for my new, expanded resort."

"Ah, man." Joe sighed. "Morgan and I were really looking forward to keeping that view all to ourselves, but it's probably selfish of us to monopolize a spot as pretty as that."

"You can say no." Kayla meant it, but Dave also knew she'd gotten her heart set on her new vision. And truthfully, it made a hell of a lot of sense to capitalize on the potential of that tract of land.

"No way," Morgan responded.

Joe agreed. "What you're saying makes a lot of sense. And we'd gladly give you anything we have to set you up right. Besides...this is my dream too, to have the whole crew here with me. One I never imagined I could make come true. It's worth having a few extra neighbors to win this big."

"Does that mean..." Tom shushed his nephew so Kayla could explain.

"Yeah. After meeting with the insurance company, I'm ready to throw in the towel. Due to the way they had to fight the fire and scar the land to keep it from all falling into the lake in the valley, it's not going to be possible to build there for a very long time."

"I'm so sorry, sweetie." Ms. Brown handed her another cookie.

Kayla picked at the chocolate but didn't eat it. "Thanks. It's hard to shake the sense that I'm giving up, in a way—"

"Nah," Eli chimed in. As the owner of Hot Rods, he'd had to make plenty of his own difficult calls through the years. "You're making a sound business decision. Plus, does this really mean that the entire crew would be moving to Middletown? For good?"

Kayla glanced at Joe and Morgan, who were nearly giddy, staring at each other with tears in their eyes as they clutched each other's hands on the table. Joe's stare winged between her and Dave and said, "Please say that's what this means. I don't want to have to choose between my blood and the crew anymore."

"I mean, I think we need to have a crew meeting right after we're done here, but I wanted to know if it's even possible before I start planning a new future that's equally as impossible as the one I'm letting go of." Kayla drew out the insurance paperwork from her back pocket and put it on the table. "I also don't know if I can afford as much land as we'd like for a spa, a reception hall, weekender retreats, long-term stay cabins, a more private section for naturists, and then the Powertools houses we'd build on the other side of that bend in the shoreline for a bit of privacy."

"Wow. I thought our expansion was fancy." Eli laughed. "Powertools is going to be busy for the next five years!"

"I still need to do a ton of budgeting and financial planning to see if these ideas will pan out." Kayla toyed with the piercing in her lip, making Dave want to lean over and kiss it. But he figured he'd save that for later when they were, hopefully, celebrating, "But, uh, Tom... If you're even willing to sell, do you have any idea of the fair market value of the land? Or what you'd be asking for it?"

When he named a number far lower than what they'd speculated, Dave braced himself.

"Come on." Kayla stood abruptly.

"Too much?" Tom raised a brow. "I could—"

"No! I'm not trying to steal it from you. It's gorgeous and yours. Don't insult me like that. I'll find a way to pay what it's worth."

Tom's face softened then. Instead of arguing, he walked around to hold Kayla's hands in his and peer directly into her eyes so she could clearly see he wasn't messing around with her. When she settled, he said, "Hang on one second. I have something I want to show you, okay?"

Kayla hesitated, but nodded, her face losing some of the pink that had flared in her cheeks.

He went into the living room and rummaged around in an antique desk before returning and handing her a sheaf of papers.

"What's this?" she asked even as she flipped through them.

"That's the appraisal I got on the land when Joe asked me about it. Because he's as fucking stubborn as you are and wouldn't let me give it to him for his birthday." Tom shoved Joe's shoulder as he mumbled, "You kids."

Dave held his breath as Kayla perused the legalese. Better her than him. She was so much smarter about stuff like that. He was in awe of her and how she'd managed her company on her own all these years. Even more, he was excited to see what she was about to unleash on

Middletown now that she was rediscovering her confidence.

"Are you shitting me?" Kayla flipped the paper over as if expecting to see more than what was on the front sides. "That's it?"

"What can I say?" Tom shrugged. "Middletown used to be literally the middle of nowhere. A sleepy valley and a town with the essentials for those who farmed, camped, or hunted here. It's only the Hot Rods and now Hot Rides who are putting us on the map. This is a good time to get in, before things skyrocket."

"I offered him that plus five percent," Joe told Kayla. "And I still thought it was a hell of a bargain."

"It is." Kayla looked up at Joe and smiled. "You really won't be mad if I steal it from you?"

"You're granting all my wishes, Kayla." He reached across the table and held her hand. "You have no idea how many times I've daydreamed about this happening even though I never imagined it actually could. I'm sorry as hell about Bare Natural, but I'm not going to lie: I think this is where we were meant to be and I know you're going to make a killing here."

"I'll raise the bid to this plus ten percent to beat out your nephew." Kayla grinned up at Tom. "With the settlement, we'll still have plenty of money left over for the construction on the grounds and cash flow to hold us over until we can reopen."

"That's not necessary," Tom said, but Ms. Brown poked his ribs. Figures, as a mother of two independent women herself, she would understand Kayla's need to earn this.

"What he means is, he'll take it," Ms. Brown told Kayla with a heartfelt smile. "As long as the sale includes a provision for us to get massages once a week for life."

Kayla laughed then, and Dave was unable to believe how the universe had a way of setting things right.

He remembered something Kayla had told him when he was struggling with his new normal after his accident, before he'd relearned how to walk or fuck. So he turned to her and repeated it back, "You know, Kayla, storms don't last forever."

Her lip wobbled and she dashed away a tear before it could roll down her face. "Damn it. I wasn't going to cry."

Morgan got up then and smothered Kayla in a hug. Sally, who was looking pretty preggers these days, piled on, shocking Dave with a few tears of her own. She grumbled, "Fucking hormones."

Everyone cracked up, especially Alanso, who was there to pull Sally into his lap and wipe her cheeks after she relinquished her hold on Kayla. For a few minutes they enjoyed the cookies and each other, knowing it was only the first of many fun times spent around this table in each other's company.

"Hey, Uncle Tom," Joe asked without looking away from Kayla and Dave or letting go of Morgan's hand.

"Yeah?"

"Will you keep our kids overnight? Mike's too?" Joe grinned then. "I think we have some crew *negotiations* to deal with."

"Are those naked negotiations?" Alanso asked with a smirk.

"Yes. Yes, they will be." Dave answered on behalf of the crew. The younger generation laughed as Ms. Brown hid her face against Tom's shoulder and he simply smirked.

14

Dave carried a pile of blankets out to the backyard of Joe and Morgan's rental house. Mike was lugging a cooler and several others had trays of snacks. They'd stayed over at Hot Rods most of the afternoon, and had already kicked off the festivities with their friends and extended family. The Hot Rides gang had joined them when they'd heard the good news.

Dave hadn't stopped grinning for long enough to keep his face from aching. But damn, this felt right.

Kate took a quilt from him and spread it out on the grass in the backyard where they'd decided to lay out, look at the stars, and envision the empire they were about to start building down in the valley beyond the manicured lawn and hedge fence of this gorgeous house.

In their enthusiasm, they might have forgotten that the nights were starting to get chillier. Dave took a seat next to Kayla and grabbed another cover, wrapping it around his shoulders before tugging his wife into his lap and surrounding her in his heat and arms. "I guess we'll need to snuggle to stay warm."

"Or we could start a fire," Joe suggested. "There's a bunch of wood in the shed."

Kayla went stiff in Dave's hold. "I don't know..."

"Oh shit, sorry." Joe bent down and kissed her cheek in apology. "I wasn't thinking."

"Wait." Kayla reached out and squeezed his forearm. "So much has already been taken away from us. I don't want to lose this too. Do it. Just, Dave, don't let go and no one else do something dumb and set your ass on fire or some shit, okay?"

Neil saluted her. "I promise I will try not to be a moron. In fact, want me to go get the fire extinguisher I saw in the garage before?"

Kayla nodded. "Please."

"I'm so proud of you," Dave murmured in her ear, but the rest of the crew were huddled around close and echoed his approval. "For being brave and willing to make the smartest decisions for our future, even if they're hard now. You're incredible, you know that?"

"I couldn't do this without you. All of you, really." Kayla leaned against him fully and let her gaze roam the gathering, including Neil, who returned with the fire extinguisher and set it close by. Then she paused extra on Devon. They'd always been close and he knew she still felt bad about their falling out, even though Devon had pretty much immediately forgiven her as soon as they'd cooled off. "Thank you. I love each of you. And I'm sorry if I'm super stressed out and snippy for the next year or two until we find out for sure if I can really pull this off and get this new thing up and running even half as successfully as I imagine it could be."

"Don't worry. We'll be here for you on the rough days." Mike spoke with the authority of his position as their foreman. No matter what happened with the Powertools company, he'd still hold that title when they were alone.

"We're good at distracting you, aren't we?" Joe asked as he cracked open a beer and took a long pull from the bottle.

Dave figured Joe was proving his point as the four women ringing the fire he'd kindled ogled his tan, flexing throat. Right then Dave was glad Kayla was so resilient she'd allowed them to stoke the flames. She impressed the hell out of him and made this possible. Besides, they were going to need the warmth from that fire for what they were about to do.

He was sure of it when Mike crossed his arms and said, "We're partying to kick off the next phase of Bare Natural, so what are we doing with all these clothes on? Seems only fitting that we do it naked."

Kayla stood fast enough that Dave covered his nuts just in case. A groin injury now would be terrible timing when things were heating up quick. The rest of the crew guys cracked up at him as they helped their wives strip before getting rid of their own jeans and T-shirts.

And then they were nude, exposed to the night air, cool on one side and toasty on the other as the flames began to build and dance. Dave gathered Kayla close to him again, then sank onto the blankets they'd laid over the thick green grass. "You okay?"

"I'll be better if you live up to Joe's promise and take my mind off the fire." Kayla shivered. Dave looked at his friends.

Mike grabbed a piece of chocolate off the plate with the marshmallows and held it near the heat. It only took a few seconds for it to start to melt. And when it did, he turned toward Kayla and smeared it over her chest, belly, and even dotted the tip of her nose before trailing his messy fingers across her lips. "Enjoy, boys."

The Powertools left their wives with hungry eyes. They descended on Kayla, each finding a place to lick her and remove the candy from her skin. She sighed and stretched, her fingers curling in someone's hair even as she held Dave's face close to her breast where he was thoroughly enjoying his dessert.

But all too soon there was no confection left. So Mike repeated the process, this time giving Kate the same treatment. They made their way around to each of the women, stoking their arousal as surely as they had the campfire with a round of kisses, licks, and sweet caresses.

Dave loved bringing each of them pleasure, especially since he knew that his friends would do the same for Kayla. They always made sure she was taken care of. It felt so damn good to be back together, and to know that they weren't going to be ripped apart anytime soon. "I'm so fucking glad we're here. One crew again. For good."

"Me too." Joe got serious then. "I've never wanted something as bad as for you to join us here. I'm sorry it happened this way, but I can't stop thinking how lucky I am. I'm sorry, Kayla. I know that's fucked up."

"It's not." She knelt so she could reach across the gap to where he cuddled with Morgan, then kissed him softly, doing absolutely nothing to keep Dave's cock from getting rock hard. "I love you too. And I'm so thankful you don't mind me crashing the site you'd picked for your new home."

"Now it will be *our* home." Joe scanned the rest of the crew. Each of them nodded.

It was going to be the best being so close all the time. At work. At home. In bed...

Dave studied his wife and Joe together, then knew exactly what he wanted next. "Joe, why don't you show us that you really missed us? Fuck me, while I fuck Kayla."

Morgan knocked into his shoulder when he peered at her. "I can take care of myself. Go."

"No need for you to do that, Morgan." Dave pressed Kayla to her back and covered her, leaving his ass exposed to Joe. "I'm man enough to take care of you both while your husband rides me."

He patted the quilt near Kayla's shoulder and Morgan slid into position, one thigh draping over Kayla, cutting diagonally across her torso. Dave kissed his wife thoroughly, then angled his head to the side so he could do the same to Morgan's hip, the top of her leg, and then her mound.

He'd started rubbing his lightly bearded face over her pussy when Joe began to prod Dave's ass with a lubed finger. He wasn't surprised the Powertools had brought more than snacks in their supplies for the evening.

Kayla petted his chest and encouraged him. "Damn, Dave. That's so sexy. I love watching his hand disappear in you. And his cock is getting so hard. You're going to fuck me so well with his dick in your ass, aren't you?"

Dave groaned and sucked on Morgan's clit. She was propped up on her elbows so she could watch her husband preparing to slide deep into Dave's ass. She looked up at the rest of the crew. "What are you waiting for? You going to watch all night? Or are you going to play too?"

Mike grinned, then ordered the rest of them to mirror the chain that Joe, Dave, Kayla, and Morgan had made. Only this time it was Mike behind Neil, who smothered James. And beneath them all, Devon faced up, welcoming

James between her legs while Kate reclined, waiting for his talented mouth to feast on her like he had on Mike at the lake, not that long ago.

Dave grunted as Joe slid inside him, his cock feeling about ten times thicker than his finger. And that wasn't a complaint. As soon as the other man was settled, buried as deep as he could get, Dave fisted his own cock and inserted it into his wife.

Kayla arched her back and thrust her hips upward, swallowing the fat head of his cock and inviting him to lock tight within her, which he did. He let their bodies rest together so that Joe's motions as he plunged in and out of Dave's body caused him and Kayla to grind together.

The wet heat of her hugging his cock and the pressure of Joe riding his ass sent him into a frenzy. He ate Morgan, using the fingers of his left hand to pump into her and spread her wide as he lapped at her clit.

And when Mike cursed from beside him, he glanced over to see the foreman drilling into Neil, who did the same to James, who was then pushed forward into Devon. His face was buried in Kate's pussy as he made sure she enjoyed what they were doing as much as any of the others.

For a while, only the sounds of the country, crickets, owls, and the slap of flesh on flesh filled the night air. But it didn't take long before relief at being reunited turned into something a hell of a lot more passionate and urgent.

Moans, groans, and cries ping-ponged between them as everyone's desire was intertwined. Each time Joe's cock jerked in Dave's ass, it made him thrust harder into Kayla and scissor his fingers in Morgan's pussy. When Mike threw his head back and pinched his nipple, it made his hips crash into Neil's ass. Neil drilled into

James, who strained, giving Devon all of himself while he flicked his tongue over Kate's clit, exactly the way she liked best.

And when Dave realized that this was going to be one of those times where it might not last all night, but the memory of it would be forever etched into his mind and his balls, he shuddered. Kayla's nails dug into his shoulders, promising she would never let him go.

His free hand flung out and landed on Neil's. The other man clutched it, and James added his to the pile. Mike saw where they were joined and did the same, reaching for Joe. Kayla and Devon and Morgan and Kate mimicked them.

And soon they were linked in every combination he could think of while they sought ecstasy in unison. Rapture flooded Dave's veins as he realized they'd done it. They'd found a way to get stronger than ever before, the bonds between them, forged in flames, indestructible.

That alone filled him with so much bliss, he didn't even need to come to feel their love and joy washing over him. But that didn't mean he could resist either.

Kayla gasped, her pussy wringing him as she fell first, screaming her climax loud enough that an owl took to the sky from a tree nearby with a flap of its massive wings. Probably for the best since the rest of them echoed her, shouting their pleasure as they each began to soar, one by one.

Dave couldn't resist the milking of Kayla's pussy. He shot deep inside her, flooding her with his release. And as he did he must have drawn Joe's come straight out of his balls. The other man grunted and slammed into him with short, jerky strokes as he pumped into Dave's ass. And Morgan threatened to break his fingers when she joined her husband, spasming around Dave and writhing beneath the lashes of his tongue.

Devon, James, Kate, and Neil were doing the same, giving each other as good as they got. Mike was last to let go. He waited for the rest of his crew to be taken care of before he cried out, then went stiff. He smacked Neil's ass and emptied himself into it. Only then did he let go of Joe's grasp and slip to the ground where they became a tangle of arms, legs, and bodies.

There was no coldness then. All of them cuddled together, exchanging lazy kisses, secret smiles, and a few soft laughs as they floated down together.

15

Eventually, the fire died and they decided to abandon the grass for a much more comfortable bed inside. Joe made sure to douse the embers until Kayla was satisfied it was truly out. Neil, Devon, and James took their turn in the ginormous shower in Joe and Morgan's master bedroom. James could have stayed under the warm spray for an hour if he'd been less sleepy and eager to fall into bed with his lovers. All eight of them.

"I'm so glad that's decided," Neil said as he finished toweling Devon dry, then turned to James, slinging an arm around his husband's shoulder. "We're moving to Middletown and we're each getting our own crews. I guess we'll need a couple weeks to go back, stage the house, and put it on the market."

"Wait, what?" James ducked out from under his husband's warm muscles, which at any other time would have been a welcome weight.

"You heard me. You're getting promoted." Neil laughed. "We all are. Bosses of our own crews. Isn't that the plan?"

Devon narrowed her eyes when she, of course, noticed James starting to breathe faster. He couldn't get it under control as he felt himself being shoved into a mold he didn't fit. Figured their wife would catch on, no matter how hard he tried to hide his reaction.

"What's wrong, James?" She stepped closer and held her hand out toward him.

He retreated from the bathroom, finding it hard to take another breath, his lungs clogged with steam. Tromping into the bedroom, the rest of the crew looked up at him from where they were milling around as Neil and Devon followed on his heels.

Sure, he'd known Mike and Joe were doing their thing. But part of him had thought that he, Neil, and Devon would continue to work together. Maybe on their own crew, but not separate ones. Frankly, he'd been rooting for Kayla and keeping Bare Natural as it had been if it meant he wouldn't have to give up his husband and wife while he worked. He didn't want things to change *that* much. He liked them the way they were. And now everyone he knew and loved was changing, leaving him behind.

James blurted, "I'm not a foreman!"

"Not yet, but you will be." Joe stepped closer, penning him in before he could bolt. "I get it. I was nervous too at first."

"This isn't who I am." James flung his hands out wide, accidentally karate-chopping Neil's six-pack in the process. He didn't want anyone touching him. Not right then. "This isn't what I want."

Devon tipped her head and listened. "You're not interested in heading up a crew of your own?"

"No. That sounds horrible." James knew they'd laugh at him, that they'd say he was being dramatic, but no...

"It's too much pressure. Too much responsibility. I like being good at my job and doing what I do well. I'm glad you're all happy moving on, although it sucks that you don't care about working together anymore. But... whatever. No, count me out."

"There are going to be chances to partner with each other. Hell, someone's going to have to oversee the house construction, the spa project, and then the rest of the resort. It's not like you'll be completely on your own. And with all five us stepping things up, we'll be that much closer to retiring comfortably so we can spend all of our days together sometime before we're eighty," Mike reasoned.

"You're so busy counting your damn unhatched eggs that no one stopped to ask me if I feel like being shit out of this golden goose." James didn't care that his objections sounded petulant when he spit them out. He'd been worried about exactly this since the moment he'd stood at Bare Natural and realized, even if Kayla hadn't been ready to admit it to herself, that there was no bouncing back from that tragedy. Not there.

Devon smiled then. "I have a proposition for you."

Ordinarily those words from her would have him perking up, spiritually and also south of the border. These days, he was afraid to get his hopes up. It was all too much. Things were spiraling out of control, one massive switch up after another, and soon he wouldn't even recognize the life they were building anymore.

"You can work for me." She held her hand out to him, palm up. "I'm happy to boss you around."

He didn't mean to, but he snorted at that. She was pretty good at it.

"Come on." She curled her fingers, beckoning him.

"But their plans and the revenue they're expecting…"

"Are still amazing, even with five crews instead of six." Mike put his hand on James's shoulder and the muscles there unknotted some. He would always be their foreman, even if they were all foremen these days. "No one's going to pressure you into doing a job you hate. What kind of assholes do you think we are?"

Devon kept talking him off the ledge, at least a bit. For now. "If you don't want to be on my crew, you could do something totally different. Quit to take care of our new house. Get everything set up exactly how you like it. Make a new home for us and help us relax when we get home at night."

Devon and Neil exchanged a steamy glance that did a lot to ease James's anxiety. He might be able to make it through the night without ruining everyone's zen. Then maybe later, he could consider what they were proposing more carefully.

"Everyone's starting over. It's only fair that you take some time to think about what you really want, too," Morgan chimed in. "Shouldn't it be obvious by now that we'll support you, no matter what it is you choose?"

James could breathe again, maybe for the first time in weeks. He hadn't realized how dread had started to form in his guts, getting heavier by the day until the burden was nearly impossible to lug around. He was exhausted and decided to believe there could be a simple solution, even if he didn't see it himself at the moment.

What he didn't realize then was that the greatest threat to the happiness of the crew wasn't going to come from within, but from someone trying their best to destroy it.

∾

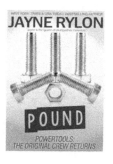

TO READ MORE about the Powertools adventures and what comes next, check out Pound (Powertools: The Original Crew Returns, Book 4).

If you'd like to start at the very beginning with the Powertools Crew, you can download a discounted boxset of the first six books HERE.

Yes, I know it says complete series but I wrote a seventh book more recently and haven't gotten around to updating the boxset yet, sorry!

You can find the seventh Powertools book, More the Merrier, HERE.

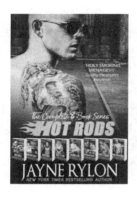

If you missed out on the Powertools: Hot Rods series, you can buy all eight books in a discounted single-volume boxset by clicking HERE.

To read more about the Hot Rides gang, starting with Quinn, Trevon, and Devra's story, Wild Ride, click HERE.

CLAIM A $5 GIFT CERTIFICATE

Jayne is so sure you will love her books, she'd like you to try any one of your choosing for free. Claim your $5 gift certificate by signing up for her newsletter. You'll also learn about freebies, new releases, extras, appearances, and more!

www.jaynerylon.com/newsletter

WHAT WAS YOUR FAVORITE PART?

Did you enjoy this book? If so, please leave a review and tell your friends about it. Word of mouth and online reviews are immensely helpful and greatly appreciated.

JAYNE'S SHOP

Check out Jayne's online shop for autographed print books, direct download ebooks, reading-themed apparel up to size 5XL, mugs, tote bags, notebooks, Mr. Rylon's wood (you'll have to see it for yourself!) and more.
www.jaynerylon.com/shop

LISTEN UP!

The majority of Jayne's books are also available in audio format on Audible, Amazon and iTunes.

ABOUT THE AUTHOR

Jayne Rylon is a *New York Times* and *USA Today* bestselling author who has sold more than one million books. She has received numerous industry awards including the Romantic Times Reviewers' Choice Award for Best Indie Erotic Romance and the Swirl Award, which recognizes excellence in diverse romance. She is an Honor Roll member of the Romance Writers of America. Her stories used to begin as daydreams in seemingly endless business meetings, but now she is a full time author, who employs the skills she learned from her straight-laced corporate existence in the business of writing. She lives in Ohio with her husband, the infamous Mr. Rylon, and their cat, Frodo. When she can escape her purple office, she loves to travel the world, avoid speeding tickets in her beloved Sky, SCUBA dive, hunt Pokemon, and–of course–read.

Jayne Loves To Hear From Readers
www.jaynerylon.com
contact@jaynerylon.com
PO Box 10, Pickerington, OH 43147

facebook.com/jaynerylon

twitter.com/JayneRylon

instagram.com/jaynerylon

youtube.com/jaynerylonbooks

bookbub.com/profile/jayne-rylon

amazon.com/author/jaynerylon

ALSO BY JAYNE RYLON

4-EVER

A New Adult Reverse Harem Series

4-Ever Theirs

4-Ever Mine

EVER AFTER DUET

Reverse Harem Featuring Characters From The 4-Ever Series

Fourplay

Fourkeeps

EVER & ALWAYS DUET

Reverse Harem Featuring Characters from the 4-Ever and Ever After Duets

Four Money

Four Love

POWERTOOLS: THE ORIGINAL CREW

Five Guys Who Get It On With Each Other & One Girl. Enough Said?

Kate's Crew

Morgan's Surprise

Kayla's Gift

Devon's Pair

Nailed to the Wall

Hammer it Home

More the Merrier *NEW*

POWERTOOLS: HOT RODS

Powertools Spin Off. Keep up with the Crew plus...

Seven Guys & One Girl. Enough Said?

King Cobra

Mustang Sally

Super Nova

Rebel on the Run

Swinger Style

Barracuda's Heart

Touch of Amber

Long Time Coming

POWERTOOLS: HOT RIDES

Powertools and Hot Rods Spin Off.

Menage and Motorcycles

Wild Ride

Slow Ride

Hard Ride

Joy Ride

Rough Ride

POWERTOOLS: RETURN OF THE CREW

The original crew is back with more steamy menage stories!

Screwed

Drilled

Grind

Pound

MEN IN BLUE

Hot Cops Save Women In Danger

Night is Darkest

Razor's Edge

Mistress's Master

Spread Your Wings

Wounded Hearts

Bound For You

DIVEMASTERS

Sexy SCUBA Instructors By Day, Doms On A Mega-Yacht By Night

Going Down

Going Deep

Going Hard

STANDALONE

Menage

Middleman

Nice & Naughty

Contemporary

Where There's Smoke

Report For Booty

COMPASS BROTHERS

Modern Western Family Drama Plus Lots Of Steamy Sex

Northern Exposure

Southern Comfort

Eastern Ambitions

Western Ties

COMPASS GIRLS

Daughters Of The Compass Brothers Drive Their Dads Crazy And Fall In Love

Winter's Thaw

Hope Springs

Summer Fling

Falling Softly

COMPASS BOYS

Sons Of The Compass Brothers Fall In Love

Heaven on Earth

Into the Fire

Still Waters

Light as Air

PLAY DOCTOR

Naughty Sexual Psychology Experiments Anyone?

Dream Machine

Healing Touch

RED LIGHT

A Hooker Who Loves Her Job

Complete Red Light Series Boxset

FREE - Through My Window - FREE

Star

Can't Buy Love

Free For All

PICK YOUR PLEASURES

Choose Your Own Adventure Romances!

Pick Your Pleasure

Pick Your Pleasure 2

RACING FOR LOVE

MMF Menages With Race-Car Driver Heroes

Complete Series Boxset

Driven

Shifting Gears

PARANORMALS

Vampires, Witches, And A Man Trapped In A Painting

Paranormal Double Pack Boxset

Picture Perfect

Reborn

PENTHOUSE PLEASURES

Naughty Manhattanite Neighbors Find Kinky Love

Taboo

Kinky

Sinner

Mentor

ROAMING WITH THE RYLONS

Non-fiction Travelogues about Jayne & Mr. Rylon's Adventures

Australia and New Zealand

9 781947 093201